THE TOWN THAT TIME FORGOT

GUARDIANS OF SANCTUARY BOOK TWO

TL SHIVELY

Disclaimer: The publisher has put forth its best efforts in preparing and arranging this eBook and printed book. The information provided herein by the author is provided "as is" and you read and use this information at your own risk. The publisher and author disclaim any liabilities for any loss of profit or commercial or personal damages resulting from the use of the information contained in this eBook and/or printed book.

Published in the United States by Sanhedralite Editing and Publishing
Edited by: Sherrie Dolby
Cover design by Karima Creations
Formatting by Rebecca Poole

ACKNOWLEDGMENTS

Imagination is key when writing fantasy and when it comes to imagination, very few can compare to the imagination of a child. My three boys excel in imagination and help keep my imagination alive. They are all adults now, but they still have their imagination. I want to dedicate this book to them and all their exploits that helped fuel my imagination and even made it into a few stories.

GLOSSARY

- Arions - The inhabitants of Sanctuary
- Blood Crystals - The first crystals that were discovered, they were blood-red in color
- Chenra - A magical metal used by Serdita and her sister Soliel to make music
- Command Center - The military establishment that resides in the mountains that protects Sanctuary
- Crim - Crystals used to enhance the power of an Arion, only the Guardians are able to use their powers without a Crim
- Crystal Essence - The powder from crystals that is highly unstable
- Healers - Arions who use the crystals to heal or do damage control such as adjust someone's memory
- Illusion Crystals - Crystals used to create illusions to help the Arions keep the knowledge of their existence from the world
- Leaders - A group that run the Sanctuary, it should be noted that Arions have never seen any of them

- Magine - A shadow creature created by the Shadow Master, Crims don't affect this creature, only the Guardians can stop it
- Memory Crims - Crystals used in altering someone's memory
- Mythrian Metal - A special metal used in the creation of Crims
- Normies - Mortals who know nothing of the Sanctuary
- Parent Crystals - Large Crystals that are used to give the crystal Crims their power
- Power Ball - A crystal ball used in training one's powers
- Productive Crims - Crystals used in daily life around the Command Center powering computers, opening doors and more
- Rotary - The magical Crim bracelet that was designanted as unstable but now resides on Telara's wrist
- Shadow Generals - More human looking than the minions and bigger in size, they command the minions and only battle when needed by the shadow master
- Shadow Master - The being that controls all the shadows
- Shadow Minions - The lowest ranking of Shadows and also most common, if you were playing chess these would be considered the pawns
- Shadows - Creatures made of shadows commanded by the Shadow Master
- Stargazer - A black slim box resembling a small

laptop covered with strange symbols that only I.Q. is able to understand

- Static Room - Room in the Bungalow where the Guardians could relax with their powers

1
———

"TELARA LEE CHRISTOS! This is the last time I'm calling you to breakfast. If you don't get up this instant, I'll send your father up with ice!"

Telara groaned because she knew her mother would do exactly that. The last time she'd pushed her luck, her dad had flipped over her mattress with her still on it.

Looking up at her ceiling, she thought about how much she missed all her squiggly friends from her room back at Sanctuary. It was strange how Sanctuary seemed like a faraway place. Though, in all likelihood, it probably was.

They were never able to figure out exactly where Sanctuary was. Lucius had told them that if they were ever needed or if they ever needed to be there that it would happen without them knowing where Sanctuary was. Yeah, Lucius was cryptic like that. He was the caretaker of Sanctuary, and Telara was sure that he knew all that happened there, even in the Command Center.

Sanctuary was where Telara, Tia, Vanna, Cole, I.Q., Chad, and Chance had all learned that they were, in fact, descendants from the ancient Greek Gods and that they had powers and a great destiny; they were the Guardians. She snorted at that part. There wasn't anything great about fighting a Shadow Creature while never knowing if you would survive. Even if she had the power of the mind, Tia the power of the wind, Vanna the power of mother nature, I.Q. the power of electricity, Cole the power of fire, Chad the power of ice, and his twin brother Chance the power of water, it still didn't outweigh the severity of the destiny that none of them had asked for.

She sighed; powers were useless against a very irate mother, so it was time to move it. She heard her mom starting up the stairs and knew it would only be minutes before her dad followed. Being a Guardian didn't mean anything when none of your family knew it.

"I'm up!" Telara yelled back, groggily flinging her covers back and rubbing her eyes.

"Breakfast is ready; you better hurry," she heard her mom say before walking back down the winding stairs. "Tiara is already up and eating."

Telara groaned. Of course, her sister was already up and ready to face the day. She was ever the perfect student, the perfect sister, and the perfect daughter, Telara groused to herself. It was why Telara liked to tease her sister about being older. Telara might only be five minutes older but, as Telara pointed out to her sister as often as possible, five minutes is still five minutes. Ra, which was what Telara had called her sister for as long as she could remember, always got irritated by that.

Telara looked into the mirror at her very much mussed up hair and made a face at herself. She'd hated being a twin and growing up with all the matching outfits her mom and grandma had always put them in. That was something she and

Ra had agreed on. As soon as they were old enough to assert their own opinions, they did. Very loudly. They were identical twins and, although there were differences, they were not easy to spot, kind of like her friends Chad and Chance.

She and Ra both had blond hair that fell just past their shoulders with curly ends that liked to swirl around both their faces. Their eyes were the same blue color although Tia, Telara's closest friend, has been known to say that Telara's color was sharper than Ra's. Telara didn't see it but, then again, Tia had always been able to tell them apart so maybe there was something to it. Even their mom and dad had problems telling them apart at times. Or at least they had until the girls had started talking.

Their looks might be identical, but their personalities were complete oil and water. Tiara was a cheerleader and an A-B student. Telara was a fairly good student, who rarely got anything lower than a C, but she did get tired of their teachers constantly comparing them.

After her shower, Telara felt more human and more ready to face the day. She looked into the mirror at her slick hair that fell around her face, complete with curls at the ends. She chuckled to herself as she suddenly thought about the biggest difference between her and her sister, and it had nothing to do with attitude.

She looked down at the crystal bracelet that adorned her wrist. She would like to see her sister leap a good ten feet or so in the air to land on a giant's shoulder. The giant had turned out to be an Automan taken over by the Shadow Creatures that Telara and her friends were now tasked with trying to defeat. Telara grinned and with just a thought, she brought one of her hair scrunchies flying from the dresser to her outstretched hand.

The bracelet was called a Rotary, a magical Crim that was created in Sanctuary by the Gamma faction. A Crim was a magical weapon that was used in the battle with the Shadow Creatures. The Arions, as the people who lived in Sanctuary called themselves, were the only ones who could use them. Well, they and the Guardians. Each of them had their very own Crim that would turn into a magical weapon.

Yeah, I think there are a lot more differences between me and Ra now.

Telara started to walk downstairs, smiling at that last thought running around in her head. This past summer at Sanctuary they'd discovered their powers as well as discovered that they were, in fact, the Guardians; they were destined to defeat a great Shadow Creature called the Magine. The Magine would bring the world to darkness if they were unable to defeat it.

You would think that having known that, they would have never left Sanctuary; that they should have just stayed there to train. However, Lucius had offered them the chance to live semi-normal lives for as long as possible, and they had all agreed that it was the best course of action, at least for now. It was like they were leading two lives. One life that was the normal one, with friends and family, and then the other life, which was a much more dangerous life, where they tried hard not to think about the fact that they might not survive.

No more depressing thoughts, Telly. Let's go get breakfast then go meet Tia and everyone at the Lair.

Telara shook her head as she thought about the name Cole and Chad had come up with for the broken-down house in which they have been using to practice their powers. Telara looked down at her bracelet and saw the crystal give a light glow. She had to stop herself before the crystal did something that she would not be able to explain to her parents.

How do you explain a bracelet that can come alive and, with just a thought, whip around and knock objects over or wrap itself around things?

Easy answer. You don't. Her Crim's glow died down, and Telara was able to continue to walk downstairs.

TELARA CAREFULLY OPENED THE DOOR TO THE LAIR. IT WAS ONLY hanging by a single hinge and was difficult to maneuver. They had considered repairing the door so that it would look better, and be easier to access, but they were concerned that someone might notice that the old Baker house was being repaired. If anyone came to investigate, their secret lair would no longer be a secret. She stepped over a chair that lay in the walkway as she heard her friends laughing in the basement. Looking around the old abandoned house, she giggled as she remembered how they used to scare each other with ghost stories about this place.

The Baker house had been deserted for many years, and the stories about it were many. The most common story was about a young couple that had lived there about seventy years or so ago. The husband was a practicing doctor, and his wife was always helping with the town's soup kitchen. The couple always went to Sunday service. They were a very nice couple from what was said about them and always willing to help out in the community. Then came one Sunday when the couple didn't show up for the weekly church service nor did the husband show up for work on Monday. When the local sheriff came to investigate, he'd found Mrs. Baker dead in the kitchen after being shot in the head, but they never found Mr. Baker. They say it's her ghost that haunts the house.

It was this story that brought Telara and Tia to investigate when they were just twelve years old and they, of course, had dragged their friends with them. In fact, Raven had dared them to investigate the property. They had entered through the broken-down door and found nothing but dust, cobwebs, and broken furniture. They'd discovered a snow globe of a winter scene with a small cottage and a Christmas tree in front. They took that out to show their friends that they had, indeed, been in the house. Rather than Raven and her flunkies standing in the front yard, there had been the sheriff with a very disapproving look on his face. Their parents weren't very happy with them or the threat of trespassing charges that the sheriff promised to follow through with if he caught them there again.

Even though Telara and her friends had never gotten along with Raven and her crew, due to their snobbish attitude, that was the first time either had gotten the law involved. Raven denied that she called the police, but Telara and the others knew better. Telara's father was an architect who made a very decent living, but it was nothing compared to what Raven's family made, and Raven made sure to point that fact out numerous times. Her father owned over half the town, which is why she got away with everything and also had the friends she did. Pulling herself from her thoughts of the past, she continued her way into the house.

While they left the upstairs and outside of the house alone, they'd spent the past couple of weeks cleaning up the basement and making it more comfortable. I.Q. made sure that there was electricity, but only in the basement, (Guardian powers for the win), so they had lights, and Cole would make sure that it was never too cold, while Chad would make sure it was never too hot. They didn't want anyone knowing they were there, so they made sure to keep all the renovating to the basement.

There were plants all around and, in the corner of the basement, it looked as if Vanna had made herself a small garden where she was currently kneeling talking to her plants. They had managed to clean up the furniture that had been there, and now it made for a nice hideout. Cole and Chad had nicknamed it The Lair. Those two were now sitting on the couch playing a new video game that had just come out on a small television that Chad had managed to smuggle out of his garage. Chance was watching them while absently playing with his earring, which was actually his Crim. He had never had an earring before and could be seen rotating the crystal around when preoccupied. His parents hadn't freaked out as everyone had thought they would but, then again, as Chance pointed out, all the guys on the swim team had gotten their ears pierced for the team.

I.Q. was sitting in a chair in the corner typing away on his Stargazer occasionally pushing back stray strands of his dark black hair that would fall into his view. I.Q. was the only one of them with the dark Greek features. Tia had blond hair like Telara's with baby blue eyes while Vanna's brown hair had copper tints and her eyes matched the green of her plants. Cole's hair was sandy brown with eyes that were the same color but just a bit deeper. The twins, Chad and Chance, had darker hair of brown with hazel eyes that had many girls sighing.

The Stargazer had become something of an obsession for I.Q. now that he knew the symbols represented words. To the others, the keys were nothing more than symbols but to I.Q., they were words that had meanings; meanings only he seemed to understand. He'd tried time and again to explain it to them but, soon enough, he'd given up. Now, he just told them what he learned. He told them that considering how the entries were written, he thought the Stargazer was probably someone's diary or journal. He found several entries that talked about past Guardians. Lately, he had been trying to discover who Zach was for Telara.

Zach. Telara tried not to think about him; her dream guy as she'd nicknamed him. He went from bright eyes to dream guy. Every night before bed, she would send up a prayer that he would visit her in her dreams. She missed him terribly, and this silence was very grating.

Between the silence from Zach and now from their friends at Sanctuary, it was making them edgy. Before this last week, they had spoken to their friends at Sanctuary almost daily since their return. Now, they would say their names but get silence; it was unnerving. Mostly, they talked to Pam but every now and then, Claw would talk to them. Telara believed that that was just to get a rise out of Vanna, though.

"No worries; I'm sure that we'll hear something soon." Tia walked up to Telara and put her arm around her. There weren't too many thoughts that were private between them since the discovery of their powers. They all tried not to be too intrusive and to stay out of each other's private thoughts, but general thoughts were up for grabs. "School starts in a couple of days, and I am sure Lucius will want some sort of plan in action by then."

Telara tried to smile at her. "Is there even a plan?"

Cole snorted. "There better be if they want our help destroying the big bad Magine they told us about."

Everyone chuckled nervously at that thought. None of

them brought up the subject of the Magine very often since the outcome of that battle was as uncertain as Michigan's weather.

Telara thought a change of subject might not be a bad idea right about now. "So...ummmm...I thought we were supposed to be practicing our powers?" She raised her eyebrows at the boys sitting on the couch.

"We are; look in the sink," Chance said without taking his eyes off the game. Telara looked over at the sink in question and saw three miniature sailboats racing around. Telara shook her head at that and looked at Tia who just shrugged her shoulders.

I.Q. looked up from the Stargazer with a smile just as the television shut off right as Cole's ninja was about ready to take out Chad's werewolf.

"Hey!" they both shouted while everyone else laughed.

"Sorry," I.Q. said, not looking sorry at all. "But Telara is right; we really should be practicing our powers."

"Really?" Chad asked with a grin.

Uh-oh. Telara looked at Tia and realized that maybe that wasn't such a good thing to point out. Telara's hand started to feel colder by the second. *He wouldn't.* Telara looked down only to realize that her bottle of water was slowly becoming a bottle of ice. She glared at him.

"Cute."

Chad shrugged his shoulders and turned back to the T.V. that I.Q. had turned back on. He picked up his controller and looked over at Tia.

"Wanna play?"

Tia shook her head. She liked playing video games as much as the next kid, but the problem with playing with Chad or Cole was that they were way too competitive.

"I'll play." Telara smiled at them.

"Pppbbssttt," Cole snorted. "Not likely."

"Why not?" Telara gave him a very indignant glare.

Chad was the one to answer her. "We won't play games with you anymore. You cheat!"

"How do I cheat?"

"You just keep hitting buttons without knowing what you're doing, and you win."

"Obviously, if I win, I know what I am doing."

Cole harrumphed. "No, that's pure luck."

"Well, isn't hitting buttons what you're supposed to do when you play games?"

"You're supposed to hit them in a certain order to do special moves," Chad grumbled at her. The others in the basement were trying their hardest to contain their grins. This was a common argument between the three.

"I do," Telara stated.

"No, you don't," Cole argued back.

"Yes, I do. It may be in a random order, but it works," Telara said before walking away from them. She went over to I.Q. to look over his shoulder while ignoring the snorts from Cole and Chad along with the giggles of everyone else in the room.

"So, is everyone ready for the yearly Labor Day cookout?" Chance asked. The giggles and joking around stopped.

Vanna rolled her eyes, and the purple flower she had been coaxing into growing rolled as well. "Don't remind me. My mom is driving me nuts already. She's changed the menu seven times already."

"Only seven this year?" Tia asked tongue in cheek.

"Monday isn't here yet," Vanna replied dryly, causing everyone to chuckle.

Vanna's mom always had the yearly Labor Day barbecue at

her house, and every year it was a big event. Vanna's parents owned VAS, a technology company that had many branches all throughout Michigan. They might not be as big as some of the companies out there but, here in Michigan, they were one of the top. They developed apps and programs that many of the computer and cell phone companies would vie for. Therefore, when it came to being wealthy in this town, they were only second to Raven's parents. You would think that with the way Raven was that Vanna would be in her clique. Needless-to-say, it didn't happen, which was another reason Raven hated them all.

"Well, hopefully she won't forgo the deviled eggs." Chad and Cole both liked her deviled eggs. Vanna assured them that her mother had not taken the deviled eggs off the menu this year.

"So, did anyone hear about the new principal?" I.Q. asked without taking his eyes of the Stargazer.

"What new principal?" Cole put down his controller and looked over the back of the soft at I.Q.

"It was in the newsletter that the school sends out every year," I.Q. told him.

"Like we read those." Chad grinned. "That's what we have you for." Which was very true. Not a one of them ever looked over the announcements. I.Q. would always tell them if there was anything that was worthy of their attention.

"Well, apparently we're getting a new principal this year along with some exchange students. From what the newsletter said, there will be several new changes this year. Also, there's going to be a new fitness class that will take up the last two hours of the day, and everyone will be divided up according to their fitness levels."

"Fitness class?" Telara did not like the sound of that. While they might not be physically inept, gym was never an easy class. About the only game they played well was volleyball. Softball was a nightmare, especially after the one time when Telara had hit a home run and had flung the bat. The coach had made sure she was never up to bat again. Of course, the fact that the bat had bounced and hit the coach in a place a man never wants to get hit might have had something to do with that. Telara was not a complete klutz; however, when it came to sports, she was all thumbs. Although, after their past summer, maybe she might be better, but she wasn't sure the coach would be willing to try that out.

"New principal?!" Chad and Cole both groaned together.

"It took us a full year to get the last one broken in," Chad grumbled.

His brother snorted. "That's probably why we are getting a new one. We put that poor dude through hell." That made everyone laugh as they remembered how Mr. Sine would read a Monday report that he always had typed up beforehand. He would read off the report word-for-word until he realized that someone had managed to hack into his system and change the report. He would be halfway through the report before he would realize that he had announced that after school there would be a mud fight between the cheerleading squad and the Glee club. You could hear the laughter down the hallway from other classes. The teachers even had a hard time trying to hold back their grins. It took a few more revised reports before Mr. Sine finally started to review the report a half hour before reading it to the school. He never could pin it on those two, but he kept a close eye on them after that.

They rarely ever got caught for their pranks. Mr. Sine could never figure out how they always seemed to get away with so many of the pranks. Of course, their school had some very cool teachers who didn't want to see those two get expelled from school and who actually got a kick out of their antics. Then there were the ones who wanted the two troublemakers out of their school. Cole and Chad knew which teachers were their friends and which ones would send them down river.

Cole looked over at Chad with a grin. "Guess we start over this year." The others groaned at this news.

2

───────

SEVERAL HOURS LATER, after practicing with their Crims in the backyard and upsetting Vanna by uprooting a few trees, they decided it was time to go grab something to eat. Cole's dad was making chili so, after making sure it was okay with all their parents, they went to Cole's house for dinner.

Telara walked through the front door of her house around eight o'clock that night feeling a bit tired. She couldn't stop thinking about the upcoming school year with a new principal, students, and classes. She wasn't too sure what was the worst part but figured she would deal with it come Tuesday.

"Telara, Hun, is that you?" her mother's voice came from the sitting room.

"Yeah, mom, it's me. I'm tired and just heading up to bed for the night," Telara hollered back from halfway up the stairs.

"Could you come here for a moment, please?"

Telara groaned, hoping her mother wasn't going to give her the famous, "Behave at the Labor Day cookout" lecture. With Raven's and Vanna's parents being friends, Raven tended to be at the cookouts as well. Telara was sure that Raven's parents never gave Raven the same lecture though, as Raven always went out of her way to give them as much grief as possible. She was one of the reasons they had some of their clothes at Vanna's in the spare bedroom. The year that Tia and Telara had both ended up with baked beans all over their white shirts was the beginning of that war. She tried not to grin as she remembered some of the paybacks they made sure to hand out as well, despite the fact that those usually ended with a grounding for her.

"Coming, mom."

Telara turned back around and walked slowly towards the sitting room, not in any hurry. As she entered the sitting room, she saw Tiara on the couch with her feet tucked under her legs, twirling her hair around her fingers causing it to curl even more. Her dad was sitting in his favorite recliner, his blue eyes so like hers and her sister's watching her beneath his blond hair. Both she and Ra took after their dad. Her mom was standing next to him with a nervous smile on her face. While their father had lighter features, their mother looked regal standing there with her dark almost black hair brushed back and held by a single barrette. Their father was American, and their mother Greek. Although her hair was dark, her eyes were a deep blue, the same as the wraparound dress she wore. Their father loved to dress casually, while their mother always made sure she was dressed to impress.

This didn't look like her mother's normal lecture setting. Her mom usually wore her stern look for lectures, not this nervous one as if she was worried about how Telara was going to react.

This had Telara's curiosity peaked. The only times her mom was worried about her reaction to anything was when it was something her mom was sure she wouldn't like and, usually, her mom was right.

Oh, Gods! Please say mom didn't sign me up for anything at school. The last time her mom had done that, she'd ended up on a dance committee with Raven. It ended horribly wrong.

Movement to her right caught her attention. She looked over and was shocked to see Pam, the Alpha Leader, standing there in blue jeans and a black T-shirt. Telara wasn't sure what surprised her more: the fact that Pam was standing in her home or the fact that she wasn't in uniform. Telara tried to think of a time that she'd ever seen Pam out of the black, tight-fitted uniform that was common at Sanctuary. She came up with never; she'd never seen it. Yet, here Pam was, standing in her living room, wearing blue jeans and a T-shirt. Her black hair was pulled back into a ponytail and- were those earrings in her ears? Yup, they were. Crystal ones; go figure.

Telara looked from Pam to her parents, not sure what was going on. Was this what Lucius had in mind when they said they were working on something? Did her parents know about the Guardians? Looking toward her mom, who was giving her a tentative smile, she nixed that idea. If her mom knew about them being Guardians, she would be hyperventilating right now.

Telara looked at Pam, ready to ask her what was going on, when Pam gave her a small shake of her head, silently telling her to keep her mouth shut. Telara bit her tongue so to speak and looked at her mom as if waiting for an answer, which she was.

Her mom clasped her hands together in front of her, which wasn't normally a good sign. "I know you don't read the yearly school newsletter," her mom began, but Telara interrupted.

"I.Q. went over it with us tonight, mom."

Her mother smiled at her but, out of the corner of her eye, she saw Pam frown at her. She probably hadn't liked that Telara had interrupted her mother but, then again, Pam was brought up in a pretty much military environment. Well, as military as the Sanctuary got. Interrupting your parents had to be a big offense growing up there.

"Well, then you know that there are to be some exchange students this year at your school?" her mother asked.

Telara nodded; she still didn't know exactly where this was going or what it had to do with Pam.

"Good. Well, we were contacted about sponsoring an exchange student and thought it would be a great idea," her mother said.

Telara looked over at Pam with raised eyebrows, suddenly getting the picture.

"This is Pam. She's here from Greece," her mom announced as if that was very significant. "I know you've never much cared about your heritage, but you are half Greek, and maybe Pam can teach you some about your heritage."

Telara had to put her hand over her mouth to cover the laugh that escaped. She hoped her parents would think she was just coughing. After all, this past summer, Pam had taught them a lot more than just their heritage.

"Tiara has cheerleading, so she doesn't have the time to take to work with an exchange student. You don't have any extracurricular activities that would be hindered by taking an exchange student and showing them around."

Telara was sure there was some censor there somewhere, but she let it go, realizing that this must be part of the plan that Lucius had come up with so that they would be able to continue their training and still live semi-normal lives. It didn't hurt that the thought of showing Pam how regular teenage kids lived was enticing to her.

"We have decided to put an extra bed in your room for Pam, and she can hang out with you and your friends. You don't have a problem with that, do you?" Her mom gave her a hopeful look as Pam gave her a pointed look; that was when she realized that her mother was expecting her to answer.

Telara gave Pam a grin then looked over at her mother. "Not a problem, mom; the guys and I can show the newbie around town."

"She has a name, Telara Lee." Her mother's voice was very sharp, but Pam just rolled her eyes. Telara couldn't believe that Pam actually rolled her eyes. They must have rubbed off on her during their summer together.

"I know." Telara grinned. "Well, Pam, wanna go upstairs and listen to some tunes before bedtime?"

"Sure," Pam said slowly as if she didn't understand what Telara was saying. She followed Telara upstairs. As soon as they reached her room, Telara promptly put in a CD.

"Oh, you meant music," Pam said.

"Yeah…tunes. What do they call it back at Sanctuary?"

"Music," Pam told her then plopped down on her bed.

"So, I take it this is the plan that Lucius has been working on?" Telara asked, lying across her bed sideways.

"Part of it." Pam smiled and ducked from the pillow that Telara lobbed at her.

"So, what's the other part?" Telara asked.

"You'll see," Pam said, rising to put her clothes away in the spare dresser that had always sat in the corner of Telara's room; it had only ever been used as a catch-all. Telara saw that her mother had cleaned it out and actually cleaned up Telara's room. She wondered why her mother hadn't said anything to her this morning if she had known but, then again, she'd kinda eaten and ran this morning. Telara looked at Pam, debating on whether or not to push the question, but she could tell that she wouldn't get anywhere if she did try. She would have to wait and see if the others could help her out tomorrow.

THE FOLLOWING DAY, TELARA AND THE OTHERS SHOWED PAM around Dragoon. They took her to Beaners in the morning to get a cup of coffee where they met Starla Hamel, one-half of the flower power twins. She'd just started that year working the register. Pam gave them a questioning look as Starla started talking about the stars and all their previous lives as she tucked her silver white hair behind her ear. Starla's eyes grew wide telling Pam that she must have been a warrior in a past life. They all just laughed and pulled Pam away before Starla could go into more detail about Pam's past lives. They told her that Starla and Starz both believed in past lives and a greater power that ruled them all.

"They are completely harmless," Vanna told Pam.

"But awfully entertaining," Cole chuckled.

Vanna glared at him; she hated anyone being picked on for being different. Cole held up his hands before Vanna could send her plants after him.

"Hey, I didn't say it was in a bad way."

Vanna just glared at him before looking away and refusing to look back at him. Cole would be apologizing for days over that one.

"Does she wear contacts?" Pam asked as they kept walking.

"Contacts?" Tia frowned then laughed. "Oh, you mean

how one eye is purple and one green?" At Pam's nod, they all chuckled.

"Wait till you see Starz," Cole chuckled.

Pam looked at him with her brow furrowed. "Her sister?"

"Her sister looks the exact same except that while Starla's purple eye is on her right, Starz purple eye is on her left. Same with her green eye. That is the only difference between them; even their attitudes are very similar," Vanna explained.

"Well, they are definitely unique," Pam said, and Chad gave a laugh.

"That is one way to put it."

They stopped at the gazebo that was in the center of town and hung out there for a couple of hours just telling Pam some stories about the town, like how their school is called "The Dragoon Demolishing Dragons." They explained that it used to just be "The Dragoon Dragons," but, at one of the away games, they had made a dragon that was over fifteen feet long for their mascot, and it was so big that it almost demolished everything. They then became known as The Demolishing Dragons, and it kind of stuck. Since then, the mascot was not allowed to be over five feet long and had to have five people operate it, three on the inside and two on the outside, to make sure that they didn't do any damage. If you asked anyone at the school, they'd claim it was because they demolish the competition. Pam laughed at that story and seemed interested in their town.

"It's a real small town," Chance told her with a shrug. "But it's a nice place to grow up."

"Yeah, but not many stay here after they graduate," Vanna said with a faraway look in her eyes.

"So, when ya gonna tell us all about Lucius's grand plan?"

Telara asked as nonchalantly as she could. The others looked at Pam expectantly waiting for her answer.

"You will have to ask him when you see him," Pam said, still looking at all the stores around them. The others all groaned in disappointment.

"Oh, come on!" Cole said. "You can't tell me that you don't know anything."

"I didn't say that," she said with a smile. "Just that you will have to ask him."

"So, when will we see him?" Tia asked her.

"When you see him." Pam smiled as they groaned yet again. Telara was beginning to think that Pam was enjoying herself; it might have had something to do with that twinkle in her eye.

For lunch, they went to the Back Bend, one of Dragoon's only diners with a jukebox. The entire experience seemed like a big novelty for Pam; her eyes got big when she looked at all the choices on the menu. There were no diners at Sanctuary, but the cafeteria always had good food.

They laughed as Pam ended up spending ten dollars in quarters on the jukebox, picking song after song. They weren't even sure if Pam knew half the songs she'd chosen. After all the wonders of Sanctuary, they couldn't believe that anything in their little town could compare but from Pam's reactions, it was as if she was seeing everything for the first time.

She probably is.

Telara nodded at Tia's words. She figured that this must have been what they'd looked like when they were seeing all the small wonders of Sanctuary that were everyday things for Pam. No wonder she had just watched them, smiling at their reactions, as she showed them around; just like they were doing now.

Jerome was working that day, and he took their orders. They introduced the two, and Jerome smiled at Pam and even took her hand and kissed it. The incredulous look on Pam's face made them all bust out with laughter. Jerome was handsome, and he knew it, although he wasn't conceited like others who knew how good they looked. He almost looked identical to Samuel Jackson, well a young Samuel Jackson, if Samuel Jackson had blue eyes. Not many messed with him; he was a football player and looked the part with his husky physique.

"I know Jerome might look like a big bad dude, but he's really just a pussycat." Telara laughed as Jerome gave her a very hurt look. Everyone, except Pam who didn't understand the situation, burst out laughing again. Unlike many others on his team, he wasn't as crude and rude, something Telara and her friends would tease him about. Although if anyone else said something like that to him, they usually ended up running, very fast.

Their tour ended at the Wolf Den on the other side of the town. The Wolf Den was the other hangout in Dragoon and, unlike the Back Bend, the patrons were mostly teenagers. This was mainly because the music played there catered to the younger generation. There was even a dance floor with colored lights flashing all around. They chatted there until it got close to dinner time. Pam reminded Telara that her mother wanted them home tonight for dinner. Telara groaned, teasing Pam that she was going to become her mom's favorite if she kept this up.

"See you at the cookout tomorrow," Vanna said before heading off.

"Cookout?" Pam asked.

Telara went on to explain Labor Day to Pam and how Vanna's mom always had a cookout. She also warned Pam about Raven, who was sure to be there.

"Sounds like Carmen." Pam grimaced.

"Trust me; she's worse," Telara said. They had only met Carmen briefly during their first time at Sanctuary, but Telara wasn't sure they were completely the same. Carmen did have the same "I'm better than everyone else" attitude but still. "At least with Carmen she has rules she has to follow. Here at Dragoon High, Raven acts as if she owns it."

"Does she?"

"No, but her father owns like half this town." Telara shrugged.

Pam nodded in understanding.

Unfortunately, Raven did show up at the cookout. No amount of praying ever changed that. However, to their surprise, she didn't cause them any problems. She actually just ignored them the whole time. She said "Hi" to Pam when introduced, but that was the extent of any interaction from her.

"Come on; I was just gonna frizz her hair for her. That's the style, you know," Cole whined when he was stopped from using his powers on her, but Vanna just gave him a dirty look, so he decided to back down.

"We're supposed to behave ourselves," Vanna hissed at him. "Besides, she's leaving us alone and, with our luck, you'd end up setting her hair on fire."

Vanna was right; Raven wasn't causing them any problems and not once had she made any catty comments. It was very unlike her. She just wandered around the cookout with her two clones, Cindy and Kim. Cindy, whose blonde hair flowed down past her waist, was also Adam's girlfriend, the captain of the football team. Telara always thought he could do much better than her; he was nice whereas Cindy followed Raven's lead in everything.

Another surprise was the fourth girl with them. She had on the designer clothes that were associated with Raven and her clique. Her hair was auburn brown and flowed down her back in waves. Telara felt as if she knew this girl but couldn't place from where.

When she looked around, she saw Jerome's sister, Teesha, walking with her clique along with a red-haired girl who reminded her of Brie, Gabe's second-in-command back at Sanctuary. They had met her when they went on patrol with the Theta faction. She looked again and was positive that the redhead was indeed Brie. She felt bad for Brie being partnered with Teesha and her clique. Just like Raven, Teesha looked down on others who she deemed unworthy and that included Telara and her friends. She liked to look at them all as if they were nothing but roaches.

As she looked around, she noticed that there were actually several other guys and gals from Sanctuary. She was about to start questioning Pam, but Pam just shook her head at her.

"Everything will be explained later," Pam promised under her breath.

When they found a corner all to themselves without anyone near, Pam asked how their training was going on their own. They told her all about their lair and how they would practice their powers, which were coming more easily. Even the training with the Crims in the backyard was going very well. She raised her eyebrows at them, and they amended that it was going very well in their minds. She chuckled and said,

"We'll see soon enough."

3

"MYTHOLOGY 101, FIRST HOUR?"

Chad and Cole were looking over their schedules for their sophomore year. They were sitting on the bottom two rows of the bleachers in the gym where the assembly was being held. Apparently, there had been a fire in the auditorium a few days ago, so they'd had to move the assembly here. Tia gave Cole a dark look, but he swore that he had nothing to do with it. Besides, he told her, if he was going do something like that it would have been more than just the auditorium.

Chad muttered, "Yeah, like the science and math wing." That brought chuckles from them all.

"Like we didn't have enough of that over the summer ooofff..." Holding his stomach, Chad glared at Tia who had elbowed him. "What was that for?"

"We were at *camp* this summer, remember?" She glared at him pointedly.

"Call it what you want," Chad grumbled under his breath.

They all grinned, and Cole smirked. He was probably just thrilled that Chad had opened his mouth first, considering that it was usually him on the receiving end of Tia's ire. Pam just shook her head before looking at Telara questioningly. Obviously, she wasn't used to the banter quite yet.

Telara chuckled. "Actually, this is tame compared to normal. We're all on edge right now. Trust me; it's usually way worse than this."

"Should I feel honored?" Pam asked as her gaze wandered around the gymnasium, her keen eyes catching every detail. Telara tried to suppress her grin. They were in a school gymnasium, and Pam was portraying a student, yet, she couldn't get away from her training as Alpha Leader.

"Just wait; the day isn't over yet." Telara grinned. "So, what is your first hour?"

"Mythology 101," Pam answered to which Chad and Cole both groaned.

"Great; put the girl who's basically lived the subject in our class; there goes the grading curve," Cole moaned. "Probably won't even have to crack a book." Then he ducked before Tia could smack him upside his head. "Just saying," he defended.

"You need to speak quieter," she hissed at him. He looked around at students who were barely paying them any attention as they watched the cheerleaders prancing around on the gym floor. "Just pay attention to the assembly."

They all checked out their schedules before Tia and Cole's argument could escalate to where the principal would be called in. They all had first and second hour together: Mythology 101 and English. They wouldn't be together again until lunch and then the last two hours of physical fitness. Telara looked over at Pam's schedule and saw that she had biology third hour and art fourth hour.

"Cool, we have all the same classes," she said surprised.

"Might have something to do with her being assigned to

you," I.Q. observed, causing Telara to stick her tongue out at him. Before she could retort, the assembly had started.

"Welcome, everyone, to our first assembly of the new school year here at Dragoon High!"

They all looked up at the podium to see Raven, the head cheerleader and the cause of many of their headaches, standing up there in her cheerleader uniform clutching the mic. She gave a toss of her head, making her dark, straight hair sway around her face. Several strands fell over her eyes, causing her to sweep them aside with her fingers. Seated behind the podium, her boyfriend, the school's quarterback Bruce, was leaning back in his chair in his letterman jacket watching her. He was only watching her because there was not a mirror in which he could watch himself. That guy was nothing if not vain. He had the stereotypical jock look: brown hair not too long but not too short so that it curled just at the nape of his neck, and blue eyes that always sought out the nearest mirror.

"Hey, Telly! Think you can use a little Abra Kadabra and give ol' Brucey a hand off the back of the podium?" Cole leaned down to whisper in Telara's ear. Telara giggled; she'd been thinking the exact same thing but, instead of telling him that, she just shoved Cole back. Pam gave her a questioning look. Telara was sure that Pam would not condone using their powers in such a way. To Pam, it would seem as if she was abusing her power but, then again, Pam had never been subjected to Bruce's or Raven's malice. If she had, she might think differently.

Tia gave Cole a dirty look that turned into a smile as she leaned over and whispered in Telara's ear, "Um, don't look now, but I think Adam is looking at you."

"Huh?" Telara looked back up at the podium to where the

captain of the football team sat and, sure enough, he was watching her. Not only was he the captain of the football team, but he was also voted the hottest guy in school. His dark hair and dark eyes were a lethal combination, especially with someone nice as Adam. When he saw her looking, he gave her a smile and a wink. Telara felt her face grow warm and suddenly became interested in the people who were standing next to the podium and who had not gotten up to speak as of yet.

She heard Chad whispering something excitedly to I.Q. but paid them no mind. Standing next to the podium in a suit, no less, was Lucius. She glanced over at Pam, but she was watching Raven who was still speaking into the mic and not looking at them. She hoped they were about to discover exactly what was going on. She turned to talk to the others but noticed that Cole, Chad, and even I.Q. were watching Raven very intently. She turned back to see what had their attention but couldn't see anything out of the ordinary.

"Let's put our hands together for the Dragoon Demolishing Dragons!" Raven was saying, but what had everyone in the gym laughing was that her voice sounded as if she was auditioning for a chipmunk.

Telara wanted so bad to look over at the guys, but she knew that if she did it would give them away. She held her hand over her mouth but couldn't hold back her laughter especially as Raven started screeching into the mic, yelling at everyone to quit laughing. Telara looked at Adam and saw a huge grin as he looked right at Cole and Chad. She swore he gave them a "thumbs up," but it was so quick that she couldn't tell. Bruce was trying to help out his girlfriend, but it just sounded like two chipmunks arguing into the mic.

"I didn't think that those two knew how to mess with electronics," Pam whispered into Telara's ear.

Telara replied out of the side of her mouth, "They don't."

"I didn't think that practical jokes like this were up I.Q.'s alley," Pam replied, and Telara could hear the confusion in her voice.

"It's not," Telara confirmed. At Pam's questioning look, Telara went on to explain, "If Cole or Chad has something that I.Q. really wants or can do something for him, then sometimes he helps them out with a joke or two." Pam leaned over to look at them, but Telara motioned for her to sit back. "Let's not rat them out," she smiled.

The gym went quiet as Lucius stepped up to the podium and held out his hand for the mic. Raven sent another glare in their direction before handing the mic to him. He nodded his head in thanks and then tapped the mic before turning to address the assembly.

"Hello, ladies and gentlemen," his voice boomed through the speakers minus the chipmunk tone. The students who had fallen on the ground from laughing so hard righted their chairs and sat back down; their cheeks were red and wet from laughing so hard. "As Miss Johnson was attempting to say before being very rudely interrupted..." This was said with a very pointed look in their direction. Telara could feel the others squirming very uncomfortably and couldn't stop the smile that appeared. Then she started to squirm as Lucius leveled a disapproving look her way as if the whole thing had been her idea.

I didn't even know what they were doing, she thought indignantly. Tia gave her a sympathetic glance.

"My name is Lucius Landers, and I am your new principal."

Cole and Chad both groaned at this news; there went all their plans for the new principal.

They heard a twitter from someone behind them and turned around to see Starla sitting there with a grin plastered on her face.

"If I were you guys, I would be putting all of your whoopee cushions and fake vomit away. I have a feeling that this one will be a bit more of a challenge for you."

"Did you see that in your crystal ball, Starhead?" a teen with spiky red hair and freckles sneered.

"No, Chet. The crystal ball is in the shop," Starla told him without even looking at him. "It's just a feeling I have, and you know as well as many others that my feelings are always right." Chet started to fidget around in his seat before turning back to the group of guys with whom he was sitting.

Chet and his gang of hooligans were harmless but annoying. They liked to pick on kids who they deemed different than themselves, and Starla and her sister definitely fit into that category with their flighty, sometimes cosmic, attitude. Starla was one who claimed to be able to read people and did so with eerie accuracy. Her sister, Starz, on the other hand, was known to be able to see things that were about to happen. Most kids either stayed away from them entirely or, as Chet was known to do, they would make fun of them because of their differences.

Vanna had been friends with the twins since grade school, and it kind of spilled onto the others who viewed them as eccentric but also fun to hang around with sometimes. Not that they were considered popular by any means, but they had always stayed together and found themselves more often than not sticking up for the underdog. The only friends they had that were considered popular were Adam and a few friends from Chance's swim team, and *those* friends would get harassed for hanging out with them.

"Whoopee cushions? Fake Vomit?" Pam looked at Telara for answers.

"Remember how we told you those two are practical jokers?"

Pam nodded. "I hope they don't plan to pull any pranks with Lucius around…I mean, Mr. Landers," she quickly corrected herself.

"I doubt they will, but whoopee cushions and fake vomit are just tools they use when playing some practical jokes."

Pam still looked confused, so Telara went on to explain what a whoopee cushion was. Pam couldn't understand why that would be funny.

"You didn't spend much time out of Sanctuary, did you?" I.Q. asked.

Pam gave a shrug. "Wasn't any need to unless there was a Shadow attack. When you grow up in Sanctuary, you only leave when necessary."

"Well, good thing that we decided to live a normal life; you can experience more than just what is at Sanctuary." Telara grinned.

"Now, if Chad or I had asked her that question, we would be dodging someone's hand, but you don't say a thing when I.Q. does it," Cole protested staring right at Tia who just shrugged.

"I.Q. knows how to ask questions tactfully."

"Well, one time they took a bunch of whoopee cushions and put them underneath the cushions on the chairs that the band was sitting on. When everyone sat down, it sounded like a symphony of farts which caused the whole audience to laugh," Telara interjected quickly before another fight could break out getting them all in trouble on their first day back at school, something that wouldn't go over well with their parents.

"Yeah, they were lucky they left Vanna's chair alone though," Tia said grinning. "She doesn't take well to their practical jokes."

Vanna just shook her head at them and then looked to where Lucius was standing on stage, silently waiting for everyone's attention. That's when they realized that they were the last group that was talking. They all shut their mouths and waited for Lucius to continue.

I don't think this year is gonna be very much fun. Telara tried not to smile at Chad. Instead, she kept her attention on Lucius who was staring at her with that accusatory look.

"This is so not fair," Telara muttered. "Why do I keep getting the dirty looks when I did nothing?"

Pam leaned down and whispered in her ear, "Welcome to the joys of leadership, my friend."

Telara harrumphed, and then went quiet as Lucius started to speak.

"I work for the Sanctuary Foundation which works with schools around the U.S. This is the same Sanctuary that participated in an outreach program this summer where students from around the globe gathered to learn about the different cultures of the world. As a matter of fact, there were several students chosen from this very school to participate." They felt as if all eyes were turned on them. "When we were informed that this school was in need of a new principal, we contacted the superintendent regarding an idea that our office had come up with."

They all turned to look at Pam who was watching Lucius as if she was waiting to see what he would say next. They were pretty sure that was purely for show; Pam had to know exactly what Lucius was going to say.

"Many of the teens that participated in our summer program had expressed a desire to experience what school life was like in the U.S." Lucius smiled as his eyes sought Telara's, and he winked at her.

Telara looked at the others. *Did he just wink at us?* They just shrugged and waited for the rest of what Lucius had to say.

"So, without further ado, may I present the Chairman of the International Student Cooperation Alliance who will be overseeing our little project for this school year: Gage Jackson."

They all watched as Gage walked up to the podium in a pair of jeans and a button-down shirt, looking like he belonged in the bleachers with them. He held out his hand giving Lucius a firm handshake before taking the mic.

"Thank you, Mr. Landon. Hello! As Mr. Landon has already stated, I am the Chairman of the I.S.C.A. Our goal here at I.S.C.A. is to give students from all over the globe the opportunity to be able to experience different cultural learning. I.S.C.A. and The Sanctuary Foundation have partnered to pool our resources to offer more cultural learning for students around the globe. Since there were only a handful of students chosen to participate this past summer, we thought it only fair to give everyone else a chance to have the same experience."

They all looked at each other in complete shock; Gage could not truly mean what he said. The last time they had seen Pam's second-in-command, he wasn't even conscious. Only months ago, he had been a Shadow until Vanna had saved him and turned him back into the man standing at the podium.

"Now, the fitness program that Sanctuary implements for all is rigorous and not for the faint of heart. However, it also contains many different levels so that you will not be tested beyond your endurance. You will be placed in one of four different levels after your testing this week; the results will determine who your classmates in the physical fitness class will be. I expect everyone to do their best, and I will be seeing you all in fifth and sixth hour today." With a nod, Gage walked off the stage.

R-r-r-r-i-i-i-i-n-n-n-g

"I believe that is the signal that ends your first period, so if everyone will go to their second hour, we can conclude this assembly." Lucius nodded to everyone and put the mic back before walking away from the podium.

Telara stood up to follow Lucius and ask what was up.

"Where are you going?" Pam grabbed her arm.

"To ask Lucius what the heck is up," Telara returned feeling very disgruntled.

"Is that how you usually act with your principal?" Pam asked under her breath.

"No. Then again, I've never had my caretaker be my principal," Telara hissed back.

"Well, now you have and if you go up to him calling him by his first name, you are going to ruin everything that has taken Sanctuary many man hours to plan." Pam glared at her. "And I might remind you that we are doing this so that you don't have to spend time away from your family and friends to continue your training. You might wanna show some appreciation."

"Is there a problem here?"

They looked up to see Lucius standing there with Mrs. Hopkins, the school secretary.

Telara gritted her teeth. "No L...Mr. Landers."

"Miss Christos, is it?" Telara nodded, not trusting her voice yet. "Your parents agreed to sponsor Miss Krios, correct?" Again, Telara nodded. "Then I believe that making her late on her first day of school would look bad to your parents."

"Yes, it would," Telara said stiffly.

"I suggest you get to your second hour before you are late," Lucius told her with a pointed look.

"Yes, sir," Telara muttered.

She grabbed Pam's arm and headed down the hallway where their friends were waiting for them with worried expressions.

"Later," Telara told them as they headed to their English class.

4

THE DAY SEEMED to fly by and before they knew it, they were at lunch sitting at their favorite table. It was the one that was all by its lonesome near the windows so that they could see out into the courtyard. It was there that Pam got her first dose of Raven and Bruce.

"Well, if it isn't the loser brigade, black cat society."

Raven's shrill voice could be heard across the lunchroom. Raven looked down at Pam who was watching her with interest.

"If I were you, I would be very careful who you sit with. Just because you were unlucky enough to be placed with this bad luck charm," she gestured towards Telara who was trying very hard not to knock the tray out of her hands, "That doesn't mean that you need to let her bring you down socially as well. You are more than welcome to sit with the socially acceptable at our table."

"Cool it," Tia said in a whisper to Telara who hadn't noticed that the milk carton on Raven's tray was starting to shake. Telara took a deep breath to calm herself before causing a major food fight; although, it *was* tempting to douse Raven's long dark mane in the milky white liquid.

Pam smiled up at Raven with a very sincere look. "Thank you for that enlightening information," Pam began, which caused Raven to give Telara a very smug look. "But I am quite capable of determining who I should be friends with, and I can promise you it will not be with someone who derives pleasure from the pain of others. I have found that, more often than not, people such as those that are so unhappy with themselves that the only way they can be happy is to make others more miserable than they are."

Cole, Chad, and even Chance were sitting there with their mouths wide open. No one in the school had ever told Raven off in such a diplomatic way. When Telara or anyone else did it, it usually resulted in a fight that ended up with someone other than Raven being suspended.

"But thank you for the offer." Pam nodded to Raven then turned back around and took a bite out of her sandwich.

The whole cafeteria sat there staring at Raven, waiting for the explosion that was sure to happen. Ravens face was turning a very dark purple, a signal that she was fighting very hard to contain her anger. Bruce was still standing beside her, but he was looking at Pam with a look that could only be described as admiration. The corners of his mouth were twitching as if he wanted to smile but was holding back.

Telara looked across at what was deemed the popular table and saw several others there with smirks on their faces; Adam had a great big grin on his. He saw her watching and gave her a look as if to say, "Figures she would be paired with you." Telara actually smiled back at him.

"Is there a problem here?"

Everyone turned, and there stood Lucius at the double doors looking directly at Raven.

Raven took a deep breath before replying, "Of course not, Mr. Landers. We were just introducing ourselves to the new girl."

"Well, then I would suggest everyone take their seats and finish their lunch," Lucius stated before walking over to the lunch ladies with a smile on his face.

Raven leaned down to whisper into Pam's ears, "You will regret this." Pam just smiled at her and gestured for her to return to her seat.

"Hmmmmm, and here I thought I was the only one who could cause Raven to turn that particular shade of purple," Telara said grinning from ear-to-ear. Pam just shrugged and continued eating.

"I would've left Telly alone; a good dousing might have done Raven some good. Maybe cool down that big head of hers." Chad smirked.

"Or it could bring much unwanted attention to us," Vanna pointed out to him.

Physical fitness class found the whole sophomore class in the gymnasium that was cleared away of all the chairs and tables from this morning's assembly. Everyone gathered in shorts and shirts with athletic shoes. What they saw brought a smile to the Guardians' faces while the others just stared, some with their mouths open. There in the gym was an obstacle course that closely resembled their own obstacle course back at Raphael's field in Sanctuary where he trained them. Raphael was the very stern and gruff centaur who had helped Telara realize she wasn't responsible for other's actions.

"Maybe this won't be so bad," Tia said to them.

"Yeah," Chad interjected. "Should be a piece of cake for us veterans," he chuckled. Tia and Vanna both shushed him.

Gage stood up there in sports pants and a tank top with a whistle around his neck and a clipboard in hand. "Welcome to your first physical fitness class. As you can see, this will be a bit different from all your previous gym classes. Here, we are going to focus more on your reflexes and endurance. There will be no sports played unless we decide to take a break and have some fun."

"What? We're not going to do any sports at all?" This came from Bruce who was staring at the obstacle course as if it was something not worth his time.

"Well, Mr. Jacobs, if you feel that this is beneath you, then you may leave my class and go down to the office to request a class change," Gage told him without batting an eye.

The snickers could be heard through the gym; this was the second time today that one of the "popular" kids had been cut down, and it had been done so eloquently that they could not come back with their usual haughty responses. When Bruce didn't get up to leave, Gage continued.

"As I was saying, this will be a test of your reflexes and endurance; hence, the course you see laid out before you. Now, your coach has given me a list of everyone's athletic history. I will make up my own teams by the end of the week but, for now, I will go with his recommendations."

Telara groaned, not even wanting to see what recommendation the coach gave regarding her.

"There will be four teams: Alpha, Beta, Theta, and Omega."

Telara glanced at Pam who said nothing, her eyes on Gage

as if she was listening to what he had to say. Just like with Lucius at the assembly, they were sure she knew what was going to happen.

"Alpha and Beta will be the first two teams up, and then Theta and Omega will take the last hour for testing. It will be the Alpha and Beta teams who will be the ones who compete in the summer competitions against other schools who are also participating in our little program. I will have the list of teams Monday morning. For now, let's get into our temporary groups and meet your new teammates. I will first group up according to Coach Brown's recommendations and, since our new classmates who are visiting have no rank, they will be placed with the Omega team at first until they are in their final classifications."

With that, everyone stood in line while Gage announced who was to be placed into what group. It was no surprise that Bruce, Raven, the other football players, and the cheerleaders were all placed in the Alpha group. Chance made Alpha as did Jerome, who ambled over with a wink at Telara. She gave him a small smile. His sister glared at her and pulled her brother over to the Alpha group, her dark braids swinging around with her movements. It was such a shame that Jerome and Adam were jocks; they were truly too nice. Actually, she needed to amend that; it wasn't that jocks were jerks; it was just that most of the jocks at Dragoon gave the other jocks a bad name.

Tia and Cole, who had a bit more athletic ability than Telara, Vanna, and I.Q., were placed in the Beta group with James, Simon, and Tish Lear, who were on the swim team with Chance. Vanna found herself placed in the Theta group along with Ciara Ford, a friend of theirs whose black hair was braided so that it wrapped around the back of her head and came down the middle. Telara and I.Q. were in the Omega group along with the flower power twins and, of course, all the exchange students who Telara was starting to realize were almost all Sanctuary fighters. Those that weren't fighters were Sanctuary workers.

Well, this was going to be interesting.

After being placed into groups, Gage had them do some stretches and basic exercises before letting everyone get a chance at the obstacle course.

All that's missing is the lava and mischievous water nymphs.

Telara grinned at Chance who was looking over the course. Gage stopped Chance before he started his turn and talked softly to him. Telara was watching, wondering what was being said.

He told me that we can't make it too obvious how easy this course is for us. They couldn't make it too hard or else no one but us would be able to pass it.

Telara just grinned as Chance took off into the course and while he didn't finish it as fast as he was able, he did make a better time than the others. By the time everyone had had their turn, there were several small accidents and many cries of how unfair it was. The last could be heard by Raven who, when trying to scale the wall, without the lava mind you, broke a nail and refused to finish the climb.

"I think I may have found Carmen's long-lost sister," Pam said grinning at a red-haired, freckled guy who was nodding in agreement. He looked vaguely familiar to Telara. She thought she remembered him from when they had been patrolling with the Theta faction and had investigated a disturbance at the Harlick brother's had been taken care of by adjusting a single picture frame.

"Chez?" Telara looked at him and saw him wink at her. She

giggled before turning back to the field where Adam was running through the course. He was staring at Telara with a frown and missed his footing before stumbling over something she couldn't see and landing on his side. Telara was rather shocked at this. Adam was very athletic, and she'd thought he would have had no problem with the course.

"Well, that was an interesting first day," Gage said while scribbling on the paper attached to the clipboard. "There are fifteen minutes left of the day; everyone hit the showers. I'll see you all here tomorrow. Same time, same place."

Everyone groaned at that. Well, almost everyone. Telara and her group, along with the rest of the "Omegas," were looking forward to it.

"Hey, Telara!"

Telara turned around to see Jerome jogging up to her.

"You guys going to the concert this weekend?"

"Oh yeah! Wouldn't miss it," Telara assured him.

"Great! Maybe we'll see you there. Adam and I will be helping them set up." Jerome grinned at her. "I'm sure he'll be happy to hear that you guys will be there."

Telara snorted. "Like Cindy is actually gonna let him visit with us."

Jerome gave her a funny look. "Didn't you know?" Telara shrugged her shoulders to indicate she didn't. "They broke up over the summer."

Hearing that Adam broke up with his girlfriend while they were at Sanctuary made Telara smile. "You mean Adam finally got some taste and got rid of that baggage?"

"The only baggage I see here is standing in my way."

They turned to see Jerome's sister Teesha glaring at Telara. Teesha turned to her brother and snapped, "You shouldn't be talking to these nobodies, Romey. You know that it's bad for your rep."

Jerome mussed up Teesha's braids, earning him a glare. "Then it's a good thing I'm not worried about my rep, isn't it, sister of mine?"

With a wink at Telara, he took off towards the boys' locker room. Teesha shoved past Telara and Pam muttering something about nobodies. Telara shook her head. After all these years, she would have thought they could come up with something new.

ON THEIR WAY HOME FROM SCHOOL, PAM ASKED TELARA ABOUT the concert that Jerome was talking about.

"Concert. You know where they play music?" Chance said.

"Oh, you mean like Serdita does at the Cantina," Pam concluded, speaking of the siren that played her Chenras back in Thetis at Sanctuary.

"Um…not exactly." Tia grinned. "I guess you will just have to experience it."

Pam gave them an uncertain look. They looked back at Telara who had stopped and was now looking around.

"What's wrong?" Tia asked.

Telara shook her head. "Nothing, I guess. For a minute I thought someone was following us."

Pam was instantly on alert. "Was it a Shadow do you think?"

Telara shook her head. "Nah, it was probably just my imagination."

"Haven't you learned anything from your time at Sanctuary?" Pam asked her.

"Yeah, but this time I'm sure it was nothing." Telara kept walking. Pam looked behind them to see if she could see anything. Finally, with a shrug of her shoulders, she followed them.

THE WEEK PASSED BY RATHER QUICKLY WITH P.E. BECOMING ONE of Telara's favorite classes. Raven would glare at her each time Gage would give her a compliment on a feat accomplished successfully. Telara felt pretty sure that she and Raven would be switching teams by next Monday. The only problem she had with the exercises was holding herself back from just breezing right through.

Mythology 101 was another favorite class that she enjoyed, although they discovered that while they would be examining Greek Mythology - which Cole and Chad both claimed they shouldn't even have to take due to them living it - there was more to their class than just that. The teacher told them that they would be studying Comparative Mythology, which was a comparison of myths from different cultures. Their first assignment was to pick a myth from any culture they wanted and write a paper on it. He suggested that they pick one that really grabbed them since this myth would be with them the whole semester. The paper was due that Friday. Not surprisingly, most of the myths stemmed from Greek Mythology, although a few students did pick some from Celtic and even Norse. The teacher told the class he would look through all the papers over the weekend and Monday morning he would decide which culture to examine first.

The boys had tried to get the teacher to explain what he'd meant about the myth they chose staying with them the whole semester, but he just smiled. Before they could badger him anymore, the bell rang.

"Saved by the bell," the teacher quipped as the students walked out of his classroom. Vanna and Tia had to practically pull Cole and Chad out.

At the end of day, all anyone could talk about was the concert the following day. The guys were jealous of Jerome and Adam.

"Man, that sucks!" Cole was grumbling as he slammed his locker shut. "Why couldn't we get lucky enough to be able to set up for the concert?"

"Well, it does help that they work at the Wolf Den, which happens to be sponsoring the concert," Vanna told them dryly.

"Or the fact that Adam's dad owns the Wolf Den," Chad retorted.

"That's not fair, Chad," Vanna reprimanded him. "Adam works just as hard as anyone else at the Wolf Den. You're just jealous."

"Who isn't?" Chance chuckled.

"You guys just sit there and complain," Tia told them. "We girls are going out to get new outfits for the concert."

With that said, she grabbed Telara and Vanna who grabbed Pam. Together, they headed to the mall, leaving the boys still looking petulant.

5

Telara looked around, startled that she was no longer in her room at home but was once again back in her room at Sanctuary. At first, she was baffled. When she'd closed her eyes, she had been in her own bed at home saying goodnight to Pam. Then, she grinned realizing that she must be dreaming, which, considering some of her dreams the past year, was a welcome change. There was no darkness; there was no cute boy telling her of dark omens or whatever you wanted to call it. She had tried not to think about Zach; she hadn't heard from him since returning home. But even as she tried to deny it, she was worried about him.

She looked up at the ceiling and saw her squiggly friends there playing around like always. She giggled and watched them for a minute or two, feeling as if she was being reunited with old friends. She knew it was silly, they were just shapes that moved on the ceiling and weren't actually alive, but she couldn't help the feeling. They had calmed her down many of the nights back at Sanctuary when she was starting to feel as if everything was getting out of hand, especially before her powers had been shown to her and instead buzzed all the time in her head. She really wished she could have brought them home with her, but she knew her family would freak out if there were suddenly moving shapes on her ceiling. She grinned as she imagined their reactions.

"Glad to see you in a good mood."

That voice! Telara knew who that voice belonged to and as she rolled over, she saw him leaning very casually against her old door frame with his sandy brown hair falling to one side.

"Zach," Telara breathed. He smiled at her and nodded. "I was beginning to think that you wouldn't be visiting me since I was home."

He winked at her. "I just wanted to give you some time with your family and friends before interrupting your dreams."

Telara thought about all of her dreams about him and realized that whenever he visited her, it was because he had something he had to tell her or show her. Apprehension ran down her spine at that thought.

"I take it something's wrong?" she guessed in a dejected tone of voice. She really enjoyed seeing him, but she didn't usually appreciate what he had to tell her.

"Does something have to be wrong in order for me to visit a friend?" he asked her, softly pushing off the frame and walking towards her.

She raised her eyebrows at him. "No, but it always seemed that way back at Sanctuary. You only came to me if you had something to tell me."

He smiled. "Not all the times you saw me were Shadow related."

She blushed as she thought about the going away party where he waved before disappearing from sight. That memory made her realize something. "Yeah, and I was the only one who could see you. Why is that? Are you just a figment of my imagination?" she asked. She remembered thinking something similar then. Could she be losing her mind?

He held up his hand in a reassuring gesture and chuckled. "The only reason you were the only one who could see me is because that's the way I wanted it to be. If I wanted others to see me, they would. However, I like that you're the only one who can see me. I guess if you were really upset about it, I could make others see me," he offered thoughtfully.

Telara thought about it and decided she wasn't ready to share him yet, so she just shook her head at him. He chuckled softly as if he'd read her mind. Telara wondered if he could possibly read her mind. After all, she and the others could speak telepathically to each other, but Telara couldn't read their minds; she only heard the thoughts they projected to her.

"As for being a figment of your imagination," he continued, shrugging. "Does it really matter if I am or not?"

Telara had to admit that on one hand, to her, it didn't really matter. On the other hand, it made her worry that she was losing her mind. She looked up to see him watching her, waiting for her answer.

"I guess it doesn't matter." He raised a brow, and she laughed. "It doesn't," she said with more conviction.

"So, um, why did you bring me here?" She motioned around the room trying to change the subject.

"Would you rather be somewhere else?" he queried.

She shrugged one shoulder. Actually, no. There wasn't anywhere she'd rather be.

He chuckled again and then smirked. "You were missing your room and your friends." He motioned towards the ceiling. "I wanted to give you a few moments of happiness." His explanation seemed so simple and sweet that Telara smiled at him, relieved that there was no hidden agenda behind this meeting. Or was there?

"So, you're not here because of any Shadow activity or any powers that we need to know about, right?" Telara asked wanting to make sure.

"I am just here to visit with a very pretty friend," he told her holding out his hand to her, which she promptly took.

They walked outside and over to Vanna's tree beside the lake. She saw Brom, the mermaid that swam in the lake outside of their home at Sanctuary, and her sisters splashing around in the lake, and she looked up at Zach questioningly. He shook his head with a smile.

"No one can see us," he answered her unspoken question.

He sat down on the grass with his back resting against the tree then softly pulled her down so that she sat very close to him while they watched the mermaids.

Telara looked back up at the bungalow where they'd spent most of their time this past summer. She was happy that they'd decided to go home, but she had to admit that she missed Sanctuary. She thought about all the questions she and her friends had about Zach. Who he was and where he came from were at the top of the list.

She took a deep breath, ready to start asking questions, but not knowing which one to lead with.

"Just ask."

When her eyebrows raised at him, he laughed. "You are so easy to read; you wear your emotions for all to see."

She frowned but, undeterred, she asked, "Who are you?" She got frustrated when he just looked at her in confusion. "You know what I mean. Where did you come from and why are you helping me?" She sighed when he looked away. "I'm sorry; I wasn't trying to upset you." She silently cursed herself for ruining the moment.

He shook his head. "It's okay. I knew these questions would arise eventually. I wish I could tell you; I honestly do." He looked downcast, and she wasn't sure if she felt sorry for him or frustrated that there was yet another person who couldn't tell her everything. He placed his hand on top of hers. "I am truly sorry, Telara. More than anything, I wish I could tell you everything."

"Why can't you?" She didn't understand any of this; they were given a destiny that had more questions than a parent when you snuck in after curfew.

"Let's just say that I understand your frustration; I have been in your shoes."

She frowned. "You were a Guardian?"

When he nodded, she found herself with even more questions than she'd started with. "But I thought all the Guardians who took on the Magine were killed," Telara asked trying to wrap her mind around this new information. Zach was a Guardian, and he was sitting here talking with her. That was when something hit her. "Am I sitting here talking to a ghost then?"

"A ghost? I guess in a way I am. Yet, as you have seen, I am still very real."

This confused her and, yet again, she found herself at a loss for words. She thought her mom and dad would love to see their daughter, who usually had more voice than sense, actually struck quiet for once.

"I wish I could tell you more. Believe me, I really do." He looked into her eyes, and she knew he was telling her the truth, the same way she knew Lucius wished he could tell them more than he did. It still didn't squelch her frustration.

"One day, Telara, I promise I will tell you everything I know."

She bit back a scathing retort; deep down, she knew he was telling the truth. She could feel it, but that didn't stop her from feeling as if she were being kept in the dark, so she decided to change the subject. "So, you have been helping all Guardians since you, uh, disappeared?" she finished awkwardly not really wanting to say the other word - died.

He gave a dry laugh at that. "I have tried, but I have not been able to reach anyone 'til now."

Telara's brows creased; she didn't understand that. He helped her, why couldn't he help the others?

"You have been the only one I have been able to communicate with. At least, as well as we have been communicating. With the others, I would try to visit, but their minds have always been closed to me."

"So, do you know what makes me different?" He gave her a look as if to tell her that she just asked a loaded question to which she grinned. "You know what I meant."

"I can only guess that you are the only mind-bender since my time."

"What?"

"Until you, I had yet to find another who shared my power. I never knew why this was, just that the power of the mind-bender never seemed to find its way to any future Guardians." He shrugged. "All the other Guardians would have the power of fire, wind, water, air, electricity, or ice, but the seventh was always an odd power until you. I couldn't believe it when I looked in on you in that room and felt your power. Then the Shadows felt your power and tried to ambush you in your dreams. I knew I couldn't let that happen; when I spoke to you, and you heard me, I felt an elation that I haven't felt in so long. I thought every emotion had left me, but when you spoke out, I felt many feelings. I wish I could describe them to you, but there is no description I can put into words."

After his confession, they both went silent and stared into the water. So many questions were running around in Telara's mind, but she knew her time with him was always short. Therefore, she tried to ask the most important ones, which wasn't easy because in her mind they were all important. Consequently, she asked the one that she knew was on not only her mind but all of her fellow Guardians minds.

"So…are we destined to die in order to defeat the Magine?"

He gave a deep sigh and kept staring at the lake. He was so quiet that she thought he wasn't going to answer the question, so she was startled when he spoke.

"Let's just say that that has been the tradition so far and is what the Gods and Goddesses believe should continue."

He grinned, and it reminded Telara of Cole and Chad when they had an idea that would cause lots of trouble. Considering what he had just said, she didn't see a reason to smile, but then he continued.

"But, then again, you are the only Guardians to live outside Sanctuary and who were not brought up with all the knowledge of your destiny. Who is to say you can't change it? I used to think Lucius a fool, but I am beginning to think the man might be a genius."

He turned to her and told her softly, "Maybe you and your friends will be the ones to finally bring peace to us all." With that, he leaned toward her. She closed her eyes expecting to feel the touch of his lips.

R-r-r-r-r-i-i-i-i-n-n-g

Telara jerked out of bed at the sound of her alarm clock.

She looked at the other bed in her room and saw Pam sitting up and stretching her arms.

"Ready to face the day, oh mighty Guardian?" Pam asked with a grin.

Telara groaned and flopped back on her bed, already missing Zach.

"Come on; let's go and get ready for this awesome concert you guys are dragging me to."

Telara looked longingly at her bed, the dream still fresh in her mind. She looked back at Pam and thought about telling her about the dream that had just been rudely interrupted but then decided against it. Nothing that Zach said was really news, and she wasn't sure she wanted to talk about it anyway. They had a concert to go to.

They grabbed some burgers to go from the Back Bend and headed over to their lair to have some private time before heading to the concert. What they didn't expect to see was both Lucius and Gage seated on the couch as if they belonged there.

"I guess we know why you got the extra burgers," I.Q. told Pam before grabbing their fold-away table to set up for lunch. Pam just shrugged, pulled out the food, and started distributing the burgers.

"So, to what do we owe the honor, Mr. Landers?" Telara asked sarcastically. Yeah, she was still a bit sore about what had happened after the assembly. Lucius raised his eyebrows at her and feeling the censure, she mumbled, "Sorry."

"Nice place you have here." He motioned around at their basement hideaway. "I'm just curious exactly how much training actually gets done here." He looked pointedly at the game system. Chad and Cole couldn't meet his eyes, but Tia spoke up.

"I don't think that's really fair, Caretaker," she told him. "We found a place where we can use our powers freely which, in my definition, would be training them. We also did it without anyone discovering us."

Lucius gave her a skeptical look. "Are you trying to tell me that no one around here knows about this house?"

Telara chuckled. "Oh, everyone knows about this place, but no one really wants to come and visit."

Lucius gave her a questioning look, so Telara told Lucius the story of the Baker house. She even told him the part where she and Tia had come here on a dare.

"So, see, everyone believes that this place is haunted," Telara finished with a smile.

"And I'm sure that no one comes to investigate on a dare anymore," Lucius replied with a patronizing smile.

"I didn't say that."

Telara looked at I.Q. who grabbed his laptop out of his bag and set it up. He tapped a few buttons, and there on the screen one could see four different videos of the outside of the house.

"I.Q. has some cameras rigged outside so that we will know if someone is out there. And…" she continued before he could come up with something else to complain about, "If someone does come up, and we are distracted while practicing or playing," she glanced over at the game console, "I.Q. also has some alarms set up to go off if someone gets within twenty feet of here, which gives us enough time to cut off the electricity." As Telara said that, the lights and T.V. that the boys had just turned on went off. "And then we really practice our powers." With that, the couch on which Lucius and Gage were sitting started to levitate.

"Whoa!" Gage exclaimed, causing everyone to laugh.

Telara set the couch down softly, and I.Q. turned the electricity back on.

"When we want to practice with our Crims, we make sure to do a perimeter sweep, and then we practice in the backyard; the basement isn't the best place to practice." She gave a chagrined look as they all glanced at the scorch marks on the wall nearest the stairs. "Of course, all the dares are always after the sun goes down, so our Crim practicing has to be done during the day." Telara smiled at Lucius waiting for his response.

"I am impressed," he said.

"So, are you here to tell us what to expect?" Chance asked from his perch on the counter, which, of course, was closest to the sink where his little sailboats racing yet again could be seen.

"Yes, I figured since you have shown *remarkable patience* in not breaking down my door at school, I would bring you up to speed on what we at Sanctuary have come up with to keep up with your training." Lucius smirked and, with the emphasis he placed on those two words, Telara was sure that Pam had told him how she had to keep them away from his office several times in the last week. "As I'm sure you have guessed, the exchange students that are part of the program are all Sanctuary workers in some capacity."

Telara nodded. She had finally figured out that the one who was paired with Raven looked familiar because she was the healer that had gone with them on their first disastrous mission. They still had not completely figured out exactly how they were going to continue their training with everyone else in the school watching.

"And I'm sure you have figured out that the Physical Fitness class is just a tool to help us with your training."

"Even with all the other students in there as well?" Vanna gave them a look of disbelief.

Lucius turned to Gage and gestured that it was time for him to speak.

"Well, about that; I told the class that Alphas and Betas would be working together and so would the Thetas and Omegas. That's still my plan, but I also plan for the Alpha team to mostly be working inside the building where we will have illusion crystals around to give everyone else the impression that the Alpha team is in there doing their workouts. I will have the Beta teams outside doing their training and helping the Thetas and Omegas with any problems they're having. And I am sure that you realize that you all made the Alpha team." Gage smiled at them as if that should answer any questions they had.

"What about Bruce and all the other jocks?" asked Tia.

Gage looked at Tia. "What about them?"

It was Cole who answered for her. "You can't tell us that they didn't make Alpha?"

"Actually, I can." They all looked at him in disbelief. "Your schools here seem to put more stock in how a person plays a certain sport and, after that, the person is pretty much molly-coddled. They are not pushed to strive any harder to achieve more. Your athletes are very good at the sports they play but when it comes to actual endurance and the ability to use their agility rather than brute force, they lack much. The only one, besides Chance here, that came close to being put on the Alpha team was Adam Logan. But seeing as I need all of the Alpha team to be you and our people, I had to put him as Captain of the Beta team."

"So, who is Captain of the Alpha team?" Cole glanced at Telara. *As if we didn't know.*

Gage shot Telara an apologetic look. "Pam is the Captain; with all that I saw from what your previous coach had put in his report, I thought that making you being named Captain would be too suspicious and raise too many questions."

Telara shrugged. "That's fine with me. I just wanted to know what was going on and what to expect. So, I take it we will be with all the Sanctuary workers then?"

Gage paused. "Not all. We need our workers working and mingling with the others to cover our tracks for us and make sure we aren't discovered. In each group, there will be a healer that can operate the illusion crystals and, if necessary, the memory crystals. A few from our fighter forces will also be in each group so that if there are any problems, they will be there to protect and enforce."

"So, we're part of the Alpha group which will be working in the gym under the illusion crystals?" Telara questioned, wanting to be very certain. Gage and Lucius both nodded their heads. "Are we gonna be working with our Crims in the school gym?"

"No," Gage said slowly, causing them to groan in confusion. "In the gym, we have a transporter that is disguised as a crate holding basketballs. During your practices, you will be using the transporter to go to Sanctuary where you will continue all your training as before. You will also be working with Claw on some new ideas he's been working on." The smile that Gage flashed gave them all a very curious feeling.

"So, we will be seeing Claw while there?" I.Q. leaned forward in his chair.

"Actually, you'll probably be meeting many new people," Lucius told them, rising out of his seat. "Well, it's getting late. Pam told us that you have a very entertaining night planned for her tonight, and we wouldn't want to ruin that."

"You should come, Gage. I think you would enjoy it." Telara had missed Gage when he had been taken by the Shadow Creatures last summer, and the guilt from it still plagued her. She felt it would only be right to take him and let him enjoy a night out too.

"I don't think it would be good for the other students to see you hanging out with the new teacher." Gage smiled at her. "But thank you for the invitation."

"Speaking of which, how old are you?" Chance blurted out. When Vanna reached over and slapped him, he yelled, "Ouch! Hey, I was just asking what was on all our minds. I mean, come on, back at Sanctuary we all thought he was around our age, but now we find out he's old enough to be a teacher!"

Gage just laughed. "You would be surprised to find out the ages of many of the workers at Sanctuary, but I don't feel offended in the least. I am 23-years-old, and I am able to look as young as needed or old enough to be your new gym teacher." He grinned.

They all looked at Pam who held up her hands. "Don't even ask." They all chuckled.

6

THE LIGHTS WENT OUT, and the music started; the eerie kind you hear in some of the spooky movies. There was a very dim light on the stage, and you could see fog start to swirl around. Out of the fog came a dark figure walking very slowly. Then the singing starting out very slow and then picking up with each line.

> *Welcome, my friends, to the town that time forgot,*
> *A town where lanterns light the night.*
> *There are merchants selling their wares.*
> *"A bolt of fabric for that new dress, come and see what you like."*
> *They go about their day with no knowledge of the outside world,*
> *While we reap the benefits of evolution.*
> *We who have lanterns that turn on with a flip of a switch,*
> *With no knowledge of this town that time turned its back on.*

The background suddenly came alive with pictures of a town that looked like time had, indeed, forgotten. There were people walking around the town carrying baskets in their arms full of fabric or groceries. They could see a chicken running through the town with a few young boys chasing it. The women were all in dresses that were definitely not of this era, and the men were in shirts and pants that didn't look like they were jeans. The houses appeared to be made out of mud and straw, with cloth hanging from windows. The music started to liven up as the stage lit up, and they could see the singer standing in the middle of the stage looking out over the crowd. He was dressed as if he had just stepped out from the screen from behind him. The only modern thing he had was the mic in his hand.

"Wicked!" Cole breathed behind Telara.

Telara looked over at Pam who seemed to be watching the screen behind the man with a very intense expression on her face.

Telara nudged her. "Like your first concert?" she asked.

"Huh?" Pam looked at her with a dazed expression on her face and then nodded without answering.

Telara grinned, figuring that Pam was just overwhelmed by her first concert. Pam turned back to the stage without saying anything else. She decided that they needed to get Pam out a bit more. If this overwhelmed her wait until the circus came to town! She would bet that the acrobats and other artists there would really interest Pam. She needed more fun in her life. When the man started singing with more force, Telara forced her eyes back to the stage.

The town that time forgot.
The town cursed for merely protecting one of their own.
Who could do this you ask?
Who would make simple people prisoners in their own home?

The man looked up at the ceiling and took a deep breath. He looked back at the audience, and it looked as if he had aged in seconds. The music started up loud and fast as the man belted out the next verse.

They who walk among the clouds,
They who play with all our lives,
They would have you call them Gods.
They would have you believe all their lies.

The man's face looked back up to the ceiling and, with a glare, he turned around as the fog swirled around him. The music suddenly slowed down.

Welcome my friends to the town that time forgot,
A town where lanterns light the night.
There are merchants selling their wares.
"A bolt of fabric for that new dress, come and see what you like."
They go about their day with no knowledge of the outside world,
While we reap the benefits of evolution.
We who have lanterns that turn on with a flip of a switch,
With no knowledge of this town that time turned its back on.

The music continued as the man stood there staring at the screen. The images kept flitting by moving to the beat of the music. They saw a golden-haired girl with a very kind smile handing a boy an apple. The boy smiled up at her with a very devilish smile made even more so by the fact that one of his front teeth was missing. Everyone in the crowd seemed to smile at that image.

A portly man swaggered through the town giving out smiles to all that walked by. He gave that same boy a very pointed look before the boy took off past the market. The portly man seemed to stop and chat with the girl who just shook her head before continuing on.

"Wow. This is definitely different than any performance he has ever done before," Tia said, watching as the fog continued to swirl around the man.

"What? This isn't a normal performance for him?" Pam asked, actually looking away from the screens.

"Well, he usually has more upbeat music and rarely does he do slow songs. But when he does do slow songs, they are completely slow. He never does both. And this is the first time he has had screens with actual images. Usually, it's just shadowy figures that show up on the backdrop."

"Backdrop?" Pam gave her a questioning look.

"Yeah, where you see the images right now, that is the backdrop," Vanna explained, her eyes on the singer who was looking at the images.

As the music started to gain more beat, the singer turned around, and Telara felt as if he was looking right at them.

Will you be the one who brings them to the light?
This town harbors a deep dark secret, so ancient its source is
unknown.
Will you be the one who makes wrong right?
Through many years they have suffered their curse all alone,
Waiting for the ones who will free them from their fate.

The music kept with the same beat, not slowing down this time. The man's gaze did not move from where they stood.

"Is he really looking at us?"

Telara glanced around at the others, not wanting to voice her questions out loud in case anyone heard. She glanced at

Pam, but Pam was still staring at the screens; she wasn't even sure if Pam heard any of the lyrics.

"Sure looks like it." Vanna shrugged.

"Think he's trying to tell us something?" They all gave Cole a very disgruntled look.

"Yeah, Cole, a very popular singer is singing this song just for us." Tia gave him a dirty look before turning back to the man who had started singing again.

But be careful my friends…be careful my friends…that you are not led astray.
For there are many that do not want you to find what you seek.
They will lead you to believe that your outcome is bleak.
Do not fall for their parlor tricks for they are no different than the rest.
If you look through eyes that are not cloudy, you will find the ones who will help you in your quest.
Who you ask would want to keep you from such an honorable feat?
Listen carefully to my words and the deceiver's identity I will reveal.
They who walk among the clouds.
They who play with all our lives.
They would have you call them Gods.
They would have you believe all their lies.
Will you be the one who brings them to the light?
This town harbors a deep dark secret, so ancient its source is unknown.
Will you be the one who makes wrong right?
Through many years they have suffered their curse all alone.
Or will you succumb to the darkness and forever become its plaything?

The lights dimmed, and the fog started to disperse. The

music went from upbeat to slow, and they saw the man disappearing into the fog as he softly sang the last lines of his song.

Welcome my friends to the town that time forgot.
A town where lanterns light the night.
There are merchants selling their wares.
"A bolt of fabric for that new dress, come and see what you like."
They go about their day with no knowledge of the outside world,
While we reap the benefits of evolution.
We who have lanterns that turn on with a flip of a switch,
With no knowledge of this town that time turned its back on.

The crowd applauded as the stage went dark and the lights went down. Their cheers faded to screams as the image of a very large red dragon appeared on stage and the stage erupted into flames. The heat from the flames brought beads of sweat to those closest to the stage. Cole stared at the dragon as if he couldn't take his eyes from the beast.

He moved closer to the stage as if something was pulling him forward and if not for Tia, who reached out and grabbed his arm with a frown, he would have climbed onto the stage, something that could have gotten them kicked out of the concert.

The singer walked forward, no longer in the same clothes. He now wore a blood red robe. Guitars and drums played a harsh beat as the singer started another new song.

Cursed though I am to walk this land not as man but as beast,
Cursed though I am to never feel the arms of my beloved,
I await the day of my release,
The day of my revenge against those from above.
Cursed for my arrogance and pride,

Cursed were the ones who stood by my side.
A curse only one can break.
Come, my son, a decision you must make.
To discover the truth,
You must look beyond the lies.
To set me free,
All you have to do is open your eyes.
Cursed for my arrogance and pride.
Cursed were the ones who stood by my side.
A curse only one can break.
Come, my son, a decision you must make.
Blood of my blood hear me cry.
Power of my power seek me out.
I will show the truth hidden in lies.
Time for you to discover what you are truly about.

The lights dimmed. The music went low as they saw the singer slowly walk backwards yet again, his voice echoing softly through the building as he sang.

Blood of blood,
Hear me cry.
Power of my Power,
Seek me out.

The lights went out plunging the room into darkness. When they turned back on, the stage was empty, and the applause was deafening. Telara looked over at Cole, who had a glazed look in his eyes. Tia's hand was clasped tightly around his arm.

"Cole!" Tia was yelling at him, but nothing seemed to snap him out of the trance he was in. I.Q. and Chad snapped their fingers in his face with no reaction while Chance tried shaking him.

"*Cole!*"

At Telara's mind shout, Cole jerked around and looked at her.

"What happened, man?" Chad looked concerned while Cole just looked confused.

"I don't know." Cole looked back up at the stage and then around at all the people milling around them leaving the concert. "Guess we better get going."

Cole walked away leaving everyone a bit confused. They could all sense that Cole was keeping something from them, but they didn't want to press him. He would tell them when he was ready and, if he took too long, they would just sic Vanna on him.

"So, what did you think of your first concert?" Cole leaned across the table at the Wolf Den and snagged a nacho from Tia's plate. He leaned back before she could retaliate but had to go running for his ticket stub that mysteriously flew from the table to the floor.

"What?" Tia smiled at Telara who just shook her head.

It seemed Cole had already gotten past the incident at the concert. They looked back to see what Pam's answer to his question was, but it appeared she wasn't even paying attention to them as she was staring into space. Telara waved her hand in front of her face.

"Earth to Pam."

"Huh?"

They laughed at her.

"Must have had some impact on her," Cole chortled.

Pam grinned weakly, and Telara had a feeling there was something more to this. The conversation steered back to the different effects from the concert that night as their other friends joined them at the table. Everyone talked about the movie that had played in the background and how it looked so real.

"So, did you enjoy the concert?"

Telara looked up to see Adam standing there smiling down at her while resting his hand on the back of her chair. Adam was considered to be one of the coolest jocks in the school. This basically meant he still hung out with all his football buddies but never participated in the harassment of other students who never seemed to be able to elevate themselves to the cool status. He was even known to step in from time-to-time when Bruce and his buddies would get a bit overzealous. His dates consisted of cheerleaders, Drama Club members, or any female whose bust size was always bigger than her I.Q. While Tiara was a cheerleader, Adam had never seemed interested. Many at the school had always attributed this to the fact that she was one of the rare cheerleaders who was also smart.

"Yeah, it was pretty spectacular." Telara smiled back. She was surprised when he pulled a chair up beside her, turning it around so that he could straddle it. He picked up a nacho off her plate and popped it into his mouth.

"May I?"

"Isn't it kinda redundant to ask after the fact?" Telara giggled at him.

"Whoa, Telara's giggling at Adam. Wait 'til all the cheerleaders see this."

Telara glared at Cole and Chad who were grinning.

"Shut it, guys!"

That only brought bigger grins to their faces.

"Idiots," Telara said in explanation when Adam looked from her to the guys with a puzzled expression. Adam just smiled at her.

"So where do you think they'll be placing you in P.E. on Monday?" he asked her.

Telara had to bite her lip from telling him that she already knew, considering no one was supposed to know until Monday. "I guess we'll have to wait and see."

"Yeah, Raven was not too thrilled with how well you were doing on the course."

"Hmmpphh. That's just because she couldn't get through the course without crying about a broken nail or her hair getting out of place."

Adam threw back his head laughing at her very accurate description. The rest of the conversation steered away from the concert to the crazy obstacle course that Gage had set up. Telara glanced over at Pam and realized that she still hadn't joined the conversation. She wondered why…

As soon as they got home that night, Telara was quick to question Pam on why she hadn't participated in the conversation.

"It's nothing."

"Nothing? You barely spoke at the Wolf Den."

"Well, the way the football captain was hanging all over you, I'm surprised you were able to pay me any attention." Pam grinned at her, and Telara knew she was being teased, but it still made her feel uncomfortable.

"No changing the subject. Something upset you, and I want to know what it was."

"Nothing upset me; it was just the song about the town that reminded me of something."

"What?"

"I can't place my finger on it." Pam looked thoughtfully at Telara. "Just reminded me of a bedtime story I was told when I was very little."

"You were actually told bedtime stories as a child?" It was Telara's turn to tease. "And here I thought you were raised on nothing but tactical battles and fighting techniques." At Pam's frown, Telara hastened to assure her that she was only teasing.

"I know," Pam sighed. "But you're not far off. My mom was the one who read me bedtime stories when I was younger, but I lost her shortly after turning nine."

"Oh! I am so sorry!" Telara really felt like a heel.

"No reason to be sorry; it just happened. Since then, it has been dad, my two brothers, and me. And yes, from that point on, my life was all about tactics and fighting. My dad works at the Sanctuary in Greece and wanted the same for me." The sad look on Pam's face made Telara decide to change the subject.

"So, the bedtime story?" she prompted.

Pam gave her a grateful smile for not pushing. "I can't remember how the story went exactly, but there was a story that was told about a town that got on the bad side of some God or Goddess. I can't remember exactly, but I think the town was cursed because they sided against this God or Goddess. It has been so long since I have heard it that it is just vague memories to me." Pam laughed halfheartedly. "I never even thought of the story 'til that song."

"I'm sorry. I wanted to show you a good time not bring back bad memories."

"Oh, no," Pam hastened to assure her. "They definitely aren't bad memories; just ones I haven't thought about in a long time. The Sanctuary and my duty became a big part of my life. When that happened, childhood bedtime stories and having fun took a back seat." Pam gave Telara a smile. "I did have fun tonight, and I am thankful for you bringing me with you."

Telara grinned a Cheshire grin. "Well, that is only the beginning. Stick with me kid, and I will show you exactly the kind of fun a teenager should have."

"Hmmmm…Should I be scared?"

Telara just smiled and crawled under the covers, not saying another word.

7

———

MONDAY MORNING TURNED out to be plenty entertaining for Telara and her group. Raven threw a small temper tantrum when she discovered that she, and one of her clones, had been placed on the Omega team. Her other clone made the Theta team, which was just another thing that had her upset. The final straw was discovering that Telara and her crew had made the Alpha team. Raven could be heard screeching down the hallway as she headed to the principal's office to file a complaint against Gage. She swore that her daddy would be called in for this humiliation.

"Man, won't she be upset when she realizes her daddy won't be able to fix this for her?" Telara tried not to smile at Tia.

Chance snorted. *"If her daddy doesn't fix it for her, I'll be surprised."* This wiped the smile off all their faces as they all remembered how many times Raven's father had used his influence in the past to turn everything =in Raven's favor. *"But we will see."*

Raven did not turn up for the rest of the period, so no one knew whether she was able to get her way. They were all placed with their teams and given their instructions, which pretty much took the full two hours. The Thetas and Omegas were paired together outside to continue their training. Gage informed them that he wanted them to work on their team-work so that they would be able to work together by the end of the month and possibly advance in their ranks.

The Betas, who consisted of many Sanctuary workers along with several jocks that actually understood the term "hard work," would work with the Thetas and Omegas for the month until Gage felt that they could work on their own. As Adam was the Beta's team captain, Bruce could be seen glaring at him from his group of Thetas. Gage informed them that after the month was out, the Betas and Alphas would then start working together on different drills that would be performed at the competition at the end of year.

It took the full two hours of class for Gage to give everyone their positions and rules. He told Pam, as the Alpha's team captain, that starting tomorrow, they would handle all their training inside for the first month. As they were standing by their lockers getting ready to leave for the day, they saw Raven glaring at them from her locker down the hall.

"Don't let her get to you," Pam told Telara under her breath.

"Easier said than done," Telara muttered back. "The hatred between us and them has a long history."

Pam chuckled. "That I can see, but now you have to realize that you are no longer just a teenage girl." She gave her a knowing look to which Telara gave a grudging nod.

It was a little reminder that she was a teenager with powers and responsibilities; it was a reminder that she really wished she could forget for just a minute.

TUESDAY WAS THE FIRST TIME THEY WERE ABLE TO USE THE transporter and see Sanctuary once again. For them, the weird part was that it felt as if they were going back home after visiting family. Telara looked around and felt as if there was something different about Sanctuary, but they had only been gone for about a month. She looked over at Pam who was grinning from ear to ear.

"Come on; Claw has been waiting for you guys."

They followed Pam down the hallway to the Gamma quarters, which reminded Telara of a very nice warehouse. There were several floors that wrapped around the center of the room with crystals along the walls. Knowing that the crystals were basically doorknobs, there had to be over twenty rooms that wound around each floor. The stairs and walkways around the floors were made up of a dull silver metal. She wondered if it was aluminum, like most catwalks and stairs that were used in the regular world. They had come to call Sanctuary home and their old world they had started calling the regular world. They could not help but separate the two. Here in Sanctuary was nothing like being in the real world; yet, they felt more at home here.

They followed Pam past many crates that were piled along the main floor to an open doorway. While the two floors above them resembled much of Sanctuary with crystals to enter the rooms, the bottom floor consisted of rooms that had wooden doors and even windows that could be peered into. The room they entered was bigger than Lucius's office back in the bungalow. Sitting behind an Oak desk was none other than Claw, who seemed lost in thought while looking at the many metal pieces and crystals on his desk.

Pam cleared her throat, but Claw waited a few minutes before acknowledging them. Telara was sure that it was done intentionally. It seemed that the rivalry between those two had not been completely resolved. *Their truce must be over*, Telara mused watching Claw with amusement.

Claw looked up at them with his ever-present cocky grin, piercing green eyes, spiky red hair, and rough features. In his heavy Scottish accent, he said, "Well, about time ye decided to show yer faces."

Telara shrugged. "Came as soon as we could." She hopped up to sit on the side of his desk sure it would irritate him.

The tightening of his smile was the only indication that he was irritated, and he swiftly hid it. "So how has the teles been working?"

"Teles?" Cole looked at Telara who just shrugged; she didn't know what Claw was referring to either.

"The communication devices that Claw installed in your Crims before you left," Pam explained. "Here at Sanctuary, we have shortened their names from telecommunication devices to teles."

"Oh, well, we only used them the first week, and they worked just great as far as we were concerned," I.Q. told him.

Claw nodded as if that was the answer he was looking for, and then he rose from his desk to walk over to a cupboard that went from the floor to the ceiling behind his desk. There, he pulled out a bowl of crystal essence. He placed it on his desk next to a crystal that was shaped like a putty knife, similar to what you would see a carpenter use, with a metal gargoyle-looking handle. There was also a crystal knife with a metal dragon handle.

"Those look wicked," Cole exclaimed. "Are those ours?" Tia and Vanna both giggled at him shaking their heads.

"Actually, no," Claw told them with no smile on his face. "They're a prototype I'm working on that I am hoping your leader will help me with." He looked at Telara who shrugged in agreement. He smiled at her and moved the crystal essence closer to her. "Would you mind putting some essence on those two crystals for me?"

Telara shrugged again and, with her Rotary, she scooped up some essence and spread it over the gargoyle knife, then the dragon knife. They watched as the crystals glowed and the handles came to life. The gargoyle seemed to actually stretch and expand its wings. The dragon opened its mouth, and they all jumped when it let loose a small puff of flames.

"What was that?" Chance exclaimed.

"Those are my new tools." Claw seemed pretty pleased with himself. He held up the gargoyle who had settled back down after its initial stretch. "These are my new manufacturing Crims. And if my theory is correct, they will help me with creating new Crims used in the capture and detainment of Shadows."

He took the gargoyle putty knife, lifted out some crystal essence, and applied it to a box of crystal shards that were no bigger than loose change. As they watched, the crystal shards started to weave together until they saw a crystal net take form. Claw held out a metal cylinder that they recognized from their last battle here. The cylinders housed the crystal nets that they had used to capture the Shadows instead of just killing them. There were a few differences from the original ones; the original ones did not have any designs, as the one that Claw was holding now had. This design reminded them of a griffin that was about to pounce upon some prey. They watched as the end of the cylinder opened up. Then, they watched as the crystal net disappeared inside and, at the end, there were two crystal buttons that appeared.

"Taking away the necessity of having the Guardians around?" Pam asked him with raised eyebrows.

Claw shrugged his shoulders. "Actually, as the Guardians are not around as much, I'm tryin' to make everyone's work easier. But if ye have any problems with me work ethic, I am sure Ira would love to take any complaints ye have." Claw gave Pam a very defiant look, and Pam pursed her lips.

Not wanting a confrontation between those two to mar their first time back at Sanctuary, Telara hastened to step up. "Hey, it's fine with me. The less time I have to spend with the Scottish reject the better." That earned her a glare from Claw but an appreciative smile from Pam.

The rest of their visit was spent in the training rooms with Pam and the rest of the Alpha group, minus the ones who had to stay back in the regular world to watch over the Physical Fitness class. Gage joined them for their last hour of practice. When Gage arrived, Pam told them that Gage would help them with their training, leaving her to take care of her duties that had been neglected due to her time in the regular world.

It was during that time that they discovered that Gage's time as a minion had somehow had an adverse effect on him. He was no longer able to use his Crim; he could still fight and train, but his Crim no longer worked for him. While he sounded upbeat about it, they could see that it bothered him. After being in the Alpha group as a protector and fighter, it must be hard for him to become just a trainer. That was why he had become the new Physical Fitness teacher.

When the two hours were up, they were all sad to leave and head back to the regular world, but they needed to keep up the illusion that they were just regular teenagers. In the showers, Raven was still glaring at them. Apparently, her father was not able to get his way, and his little girl still remained in the Theta group. They all wished they could have been a fly on the wall for that discussion.

THE REST OF THE WEEK PASSED PRETTY MUCH THE SAME WAY. THEY went to school, put up with Raven and all the jocks giving them grief because of the ranks in P.E., and visited Sanctuary. Raven went as far as to imply that Telara had been giving favors to Gage. That remark had them all holding Telara back before she could physically attack her. Lucius always managed to suddenly appear at these times, but Telara was hoping for a time when he didn't. Vanna telling her that Raven was just jealous didn't help at all. Telara was getting sick of all the snide innuendos and name calling. The only saving grace was the two hours they got to spend at Sanctuary.

On one of their visits to Sanctuary, they learned that many of the mythical creatures that resided in and around the town of Tellus had managed to procure positions at Sanctuary. Pam told Telara that after they realized the mythicals could actually defend themselves, they were more than welcome in Sanctuary. Of course, Lucius had been trying to get Ira to see that for many years, Pam informed them. Now, Ira had no choice but to accept that Lucius was right. Apparently, that wasn't sitting well with Ira, who they had yet to see.

They were introduced to Fritz, the little guy who they'd seen driving the tiny car in the battle that had taken place in Sanctuary where Gage had been finally freed along with some other creatures that had been turned to Shadows. He is a sprite, which is a cousin to the fairies that inhabited Sanctuary.

Good luck getting them to admit that, though. When Cole had pointed that out to Flash, the fairy they had met during their first week at Sanctuary, it wasn't an hour later that he found spiders in his shoes. That had been the last time he took them off while at Sanctuary.

Fritz was the messenger for Sanctuary; some found amusement in this while others felt irritation. He would zoom around Sanctuary in his car delivering messages and woe to anyone that didn't get out of his way quickly enough. One time, Chance wasn't paying attention and ended up in a garbage can. Chad didn't help the situation by taking out his phone and quickly snapping pictures. Other sprites could be seen working with Maintenance as they seemed to have a head for fixing things that were broken. Flash always muttered that it was because they were always breaking everything.

For their part, the fairies found that working with the surveillance team was right up their alley. The fairies had very sharp eyes and could detect minor details that the regular human eye just couldn't.

They set up a schedule for their P.E. class where during the first hour they would practice with their Crims in the training room along with any fighting techniques that Pam thought they needed to work on. During the last hour they were there, they would visit and learn everything they could about Sanctuary. During that time, Pam always disappeared for "Alpha Leader duties" as she put it. I.Q. seemed to find Claw's workshop very interesting. Vanna, who found Claw to be a major irritant, refused to go in there, so they would wander around Sanctuary with her.

TELARA, WHO THOUGHT THAT ALL THE SANCTUARY WORKERS WHO came to Dragoon were supposed to be exchange students, found out how wrong she was. That Friday, Sapphire came to them and told them they needed to tell their parents that she was having a sleepover at her house and they were all invited.

"Us too?" I.Q. spoke up.

"Yes," she replied, giving them all pieces of paper. "These are the invitations to give your parents, and it explains every-thing. The boys and girls, of course, won't be sleeping in the same room, and it will be chaperoned." She laughed at their very confused expressions before explaining that she hadn't come as an exchange student, rather as a new student who just moved here. "You can tell your parents that it's a get together so that I can meet my fellow students."

"Are all students invited?" Telara asked wrinkling her nose thinking about Raven and her clones.

"Of course not," Sapphire scoffed. "But you don't have to tell your parents that."

"Not a problem for me," Telara assured her. "So exactly what are we gonna be doing?"

Sapphire smiled at them. "You'll see," she said cryptically before she walked away.

"That has got to be a Sanctuary thing," Telara grumbled to the others who just nodded in agreement. They hated the fact that they never got any real answers from anyone. They were always told, "You will see" as if that explained anything.

8

———

TELARA'S MOM was thrilled about Telara going to the sleepover, although, to Telara's complete embarrassment, she did call Sapphire's parents to verify that the girls and guys would be sleeping separately and that they would be there to chaperone.

"Geesh, mom, don't you trust me?" Telara groused at her.

"Of course, I do, dear." Her mother smiled at her. Her mother had asked her many times who else was invited, and Telara had finally told her just to ask Sapphire's mom. "I did, and she told me that Sapphire had invited all the kids who seemed nice to her."

"Well then, there ya go."

"Yeah, Sapphire gave me an invitation also," Tiara informed them from her position at Telara's door.

Telara looked at her quickly. "You're going too?" She and Tiara may not be the best of friends, but they were twins and sisters and got along well enough. She just didn't think she would be able to sneak away to Sanctuary with her sister there.

Tiara stuck her tongue out at Telara's tone. "No, I'm not

going. The cheerleaders are all having a sleepover at Raven's this weekend to practice."

Telara tried to hold back a grin but failed. Tiara just wrinkled her nose at her. Tiara didn't care for Raven much but, with her being the cheerleading captain, she had no choice but to deal with her. Tiara had to remind Raven numerous times that Telara was her sister but, even then, Raven would still take digs at Telara, which always irked Tiara greatly.

Everyone had long stopped questioning how they could be identical twins yet have not only different friends but also different personalities. Tiara had always been very girly and loved cheerleading while Telara just liked hanging with her friends and irritating the popular kids.

"Sorry, Ra; I know that she gives you a hard time for being my sister," Telara said.

And Telara was indeed sorry; her sister wasn't like Raven or even Teesha, even if she did hang with many of the popular kids.

Tiara just shrugged her shoulders and disappeared into her room to get ready for her weekend. Pam and Telara finished packing and then bid her parents goodbye.

"PAM! PAM!" UPON ARRIVING AT SANCTUARY, THEY TURNED TO see a bronze-haired guy running down the hallway yelling. He was wearing a uniform that signified he was part of the Delta faction, the faction that was in charge of monitoring the Shadow activity and going after rogue Sanctuary workers. They hadn't yet met anyone from that faction, so they were all pretty interested in who this person running after Pam was.

Pam turned to acknowledge the guy. "Hello, Zeke."

"Zeke? As in Commander of the Delta faction?" Tia asked watching Zeke with interest. Telara looked over to see Cole glaring at Zeke, whose skin was almost as bronze as his hair.

Zeke tipped an imaginary hat towards her in acknowledgment before turning back to Pam. "We have it," he informed her excitedly.

"You got the location?" Pam's eyes lit up with what looked like anticipation.

"Yup."

"Am I the only one lost here?" Chance looked around to see everyone wearing the same confused expression.

"We'll meet you in your office in five minutes." Zeke nodded towards Pam then, with a jaunty wave to the Guardians, he took off down the hallway.

They all looked at Pam who was just grinning.

"Would you all like to go on a mission with me?" Pam asked them.

"Mission?" Telara was not exactly sure what was going on, but Pam's smile was becoming infectious.

"Yeah, a secret mission that very few around here know about," Pam said in a serious undertone. They just shrugged at her and told her to lead the way.

The Delta faction's headquarters reminded them of the Command Center with all the computers spread out on tables and the huge screens positioned along the walls around the main room. Rather than the rooms wrapping around the entire main room, they were all along one wall. There were two floors above the main floor with walkways and stairs. There were crystals along the walls signifying where the rooms were. The main floor had only three crystals along the wall.

They watched as Pam grabbed the center crystal which opened to an office with crystal chairs and dark purple cushions. Behind the crystal desk, Zeke was sitting looking at one of the three screens situated around his desk. He looked up as they entered and gestured for them to take seats. Tia took the seat closest to the desk while Telara grabbed the one next to her. Pam sat on the edge of the desk in the only spot not covered with papers while the others sat on the long couch that was situated across from the desk.

Zeke looked at Pam. "Have you filled them in yet?"

Pam shook her head with a bit of a grimace. "I didn't want to say anything until I was sure no one would be able to overhear."

"I think we might just be getting into something very sneaky-like." Cole grinned at them.

"Right up our alley." Chad leaned forward with a gleam in his eyes.

"Remember when I told you about how that song reminded me of a bedtime story?" Pam asked Telara who nodded in response. Telara had already told the others about their conversation, so they understood the question just not the destination of this conversation. "Well, Zeke is one of our history buffs, you could say."

"Could say?" Zeke gave her an affronted look.

"Can say," Pam corrected herself and then continued. "He also remembered the story and decided to do some investigating." She looked at Zeke and nodded, letting him know he could take over the explanation.

Zeke cleared his throat. "Let's just say that the song your singer was singing is basically about a town that was cursed long ago. That town is the topic of a myth that has been told again and again throughout the years. I'm not sure if the story that has been told is an accurate description of what happened or just a story as everyone has been led to believe."

"Why do we even care?" I.Q. queried. "I thought our mission in life was to train to be able to defeat the Magine that was due to wake up? What has this town got to do with that?"

"Did any of you notice the markings on the houses from that video that was shown during the concert?" Pam asked them.

They shrugged their shoulders since they really hadn't. All they had noticed was that the houses looked old. Pam nodded as if she'd expected that. She grabbed a book off Zeke's desk and opened it up and showing them a picture of a tree with a symbol carved into it.

"Hey, Telly! That's one of the symbols that you showed us. You know the ones that you said were on your ceiling in the bungalow?" Cole said eyeing it.

"Yeah, that's the one I always connected with you." Telara realized it was the one symbol that resembled a flame.

"That's the symbol that is associated with the bedtime story of the town that time forgot," Pam told them.

"Or the cursed town as some others have called it," Zeke added.

"Also, this is the symbol that was on all the buildings that we saw in that video," Pam said.

It surprised Telara that she hadn't noticed that. These were symbols that she had seen many times throughout the summer and had doodled all over her school notebooks. She felt as if that was something that she should have caught.

As if reading her mind, Pam went on to say, "You probably didn't notice it due to the fact that it wasn't really highlighted in the video; the video seemed to revolve around the people more. However, it's because of that symbol that I think maybe this might be worth investigating. Maybe there's something there to learn about your powers and maybe even how to defeat the Magine without us losing anyone."

Pam's voice seemed to break over the last two words, and they weren't really sure what to say to that. They had grown close to the Alpha Leader in the past several months; none of them talked about what the outcome of the final battle could be. They were training to fight this creature without thinking about the outcome and here Pam was trying to find a way for the outcome to be different for them than it had been for the ones that had come before.

Not once had they been told that they would perish in the battle, but no one denied it. Telara thought about her dream talk with Zach; she still hadn't told anyone about it. Now wasn't the time either.

"But we don't even know where this town is," Telara protested.

Pam smiled at Zeke who just grinned back. "We might have an idea," she replied.

"Might?" Vanna looked at them.

"Well, Zeke knows the story by heart and has managed to get a hold of the video from the concert," Pam said hesitantly. They were fairly certain that they didn't want to know how he'd managed to get a hold of the video, so they just nodded.

"Many Sanctuary historians have searched for the cursed town to either prove or disapprove its existence. However, no one was able to discover the whereabouts," Zeke told them.

"So, if no one was able to discover the location how are we going to get there?" Chance asked.

"The video from the concert," Zeke answered simply to which they looked more confused. "No one had a video such as this or else I believe that they could've discovered the town."

The screen behind them came on and there on that screen was the video from the concert. Now that they knew what they were looking for, they saw the symbol of the flame on the houses. But that wasn't what Zeke was pointing at; he was pointing at an ax that was mounted on a wall along with other decorative weapons. They didn't look like anything that could possibly be used in actual battle.

"That ax is called a Labrys; it's a double-edged ax," Zeke informed them.

"That doesn't look like anything special," Cole told him. "I doubt it would even hold up in battle."

"Probably because that Labrys wasn't created for battle," Zeke told him. "Most likely, that Labrys was created for ceremonial purposes. The Labrys has always been associated with the Minoan civilization, specifically with regards to the worship of a Goddess. There are some that have been recovered at the Palace of Knossos and are considered to be the symbol of King Minos."

"So, you're saying that this town is located on the island of Crete?" I.Q. asked him.

"Actually, I think it's located on an island off the coast of Crete by Knossos," Zeke told him. "An island that no one of the outside world even knows exists. Our historians call this the Nameless Isle."

"Nameless Isle?" asked I.Q.

Zeke looked at I.Q. and explained, "Long ago, the Sanctuary in Greece discovered an island just off the coast of Knossos. It is uninhabited. Upon further investigation, they discovered that not only has there never been any record of it, but that it also showed that no mortal had ever stepped foot upon it. They have never been able to discover what magic protects the island from mortal eyes. Eventually, they named it the Nameless Isle, and they have sent many expeditions there with no discovery of any life living there. As far as I can tell, it has been centuries since anyone from Sanctuary has even been back to the island."

"If they didn't discover anything on that island what makes you think we will?" Telara was very curious, intrigued even.

"I believe that the reason that they never discovered anything on that island is because they didn't know what they were seeking," Zeke told them.

"And we do?"

"The song says if you look through eyes that are not cloudy you will find what you seek."

Telara groaned. "Not you, too."

Zeke looked at her confused.

"Ever since the singer sung the song 'Seven of Seven,' Cole has sworn that the singer is singing songs about us."

Zeke shrugged. "He may be." He chuckled at Telara's glare. "There are many out there that carry the gifts of the Gods. They may not be as pronounced as yours, but they still carry them. This singer may have the gift of prophecy, and this is his outlet."

"Ha!" Cole pointed to both Telara and Tia.

Zeke stood up. "There is only one way to find out; that is, if you're all willing of course."

"Willing to do what exactly?" Vanna asked him.

"Travel to the Nameless Isle and see if you can discover The Town that Time Forgot," Zeke told them. "We will transport you there tomorrow, then you'll take a hike around the island. If you don't find the town, then there is no harm done, and you'll be back here by dinnertime tomorrow."

"And if we do find something?" Cole was sitting on the

edge of his seat. He had been laughed at by all of them for trying to convince them that the singer was singing songs about them; if there was even a small possibility to prove that he was right, there was no way he was going to pass that up.

"Then maybe you can be the ones to break this curse they are under and make the most historical find in Sanctuary history." Zeke sat back in his chair with his hands connected behind his head. "The choice is yours."

Cole turned to the rest. "Come on, guys! Please say you'll go." The pleading look in his eyes was worse than looking into the sad eyes of a puppy. They all looked at each other for a minute or two before finally nodding in acquiescence. "Yes!" Cole jumped out of his seat then looked at Zeke. "When do we leave?"

"Tomorrow after breakfast. We'll have to get you guys and Pam geared up and ready. Meet here in my office so you can use my personal transporter; it's the only one that can't be traced. Remember, this isn't sanctioned by Sanctuary as a mission, so you can't tell anyone what you're doing. The only two you will be in contact with will be Claw and myself; the other factions will be doing their best to keep Ira and Lucius from discovering your whereabouts. If you discover the town, then we will bring them in but not before."

"I take it that they wouldn't approve?" Vanna looked vaguely amused at this.

"Well, they might not consider it worth the effort of the Guardians to be hiking around an uninhabited island looking for ghosts." Zeke grinned. "The leaders weren't thrilled with all the new ideas and changes that resulted from your last battle with the Shadows."

"But they were all good changes; why would they think that was a bad thing?" Vanna asked.

"They never said it was a bad thing," Pam corrected. "Just that it was unnecessary for the Guardians to be part of. They are from old times and so are their beliefs."

"They believe that the Guardians are here to train for the final battle with the Magine and nothing more," Telara finished for her.

"Exactly. They have informed Ira and Lucius that all your training is to be per protocol from now on. Therefore, any veering away from protocol is to be discouraged." Pam shrugged. They knew that Pam respected Ira, the head of the Command Center, but, to them, he seemed like a man who liked power and didn't like anyone who disagreed with him. From what they just said about the leaders, it made them wonder if Ira wasn't related to them as well. Could be how he got his position.

"And 'Miss By-the-Book,' doesn't agree?" Telara couldn't help but tease.

Pam gave a little laugh. "This summer you guys taught me that you are not like the previous Guardians, that it isn't a bad thing to think outside the box. If we went by protocol, Gage would be lost to us, and I owe you more than you know for that."

They didn't know exactly what to say to that, so they just asked where they would be sleeping for the night. They were rather excited to hear that they would be sleeping in the bungalow and meeting Pam in the cafeteria for breakfast before joining Zeke back here to start their undercover mission.

TELARA WAS HAPPY TO SEE HER SQUIGGLY FRIENDS WERE STILL ON

her ceiling and still frolicking around like baby kittens. She was not sure how long she laid there staring at them before a motion by the door caught her attention. She turned over to see Zach standing there just watching her.

"I take it I am sleeping." She smiled at him. When he did not answer, she took a closer look and saw that he looked very sad. "What is wrong?"

"You are heading into danger," He stated glumly.

Telara couldn't stop the snort at that remark. "Isn't that a daily occurrence for Guardians?"

"This time it is different." He gave her a look that made her feel as if she were losing him.

"What do you mean?"

His tone sounded so ominous that it sent chills down her spine, and not in the good way. "If you choose to go down this path, you will awaken the Sleepers who were never meant to be woken. When that happens, your destiny will be changed forever."

Telara could only think that considering their first destiny was to give their lives so that they may be able to defeat the Magine, a change in their destiny had to be a good thing.

Zach gave her a sad smile, slowly shaking his head as if hearing her thoughts. "If you start down this path, you will have a chance to change your destiny for the better, but you also chance gaining more enemies than you already have. The Shadows are not the only dark things out there; however, right now, they are the only ones you have to face."

"Are you telling me not to go?"

Zach shook his head. "That is not for me to decide."

"But you are here to help me, you said so yourself. You are kinda like my guide," Telara protested.

Zach approached her bed and sat softly beside her. "I will

always do what I can to help you; I will never leave you if I can help it. But I will also never tell you what you should do, especially when it is your destiny that will be changed. Only you can make that choice."

"Can you tell me if our destiny will be changed for the worse?"

"I can't answer that," Zach told her. "While it will definitely change your destiny, it could be for the better or it could be for the worse; it really depends on your point of view."

Telara covered her face with her hands and screamed in frustration. "I hate riddles!"

Zach chuckled at her frustration. He grabbed her hands and pulled them away from her face. "You will make the right choice. I have faith in you."

He got up from the bed and started to walk out of the room before she stopped him. "If we go on this mission will we find that town?"

"Yes," Zach told her without turning around.

"Will we be able to save the town from the curse?"

"Yes." He still did not turn around.

"Will anything bad happen?"

He turned around and faced her before saying, "I can tell you that you will set free a prisoner who has been wrongfully imprisoned but, in doing so, you will lose something that you never knew you had."

He shimmered from view before she could question him more.

9

―――――

THE NEXT MORNING while eating breakfast in the cafeteria, Telara finally broke down and told the others about both of her dream talks with Zach.

"Zach was a Guardian?" Chad's eyes got big, and Telara nodded.

"Did he actually come out and say he was?" Pam asked.

Telara frowned at her. "Well he didn't deny it." Telara crossed her arms defensively.

"But neither did he acknowledge it from what you said," Pam pushed.

Telara had nothing to say to that; Pam was right. But it didn't mean she had to like it.

"You told me that Zach has always helped you and that he has never lied to you, correct?" Pam asked.

They all looked at Pam, not sure where she was going. Telara nodded at her.

"Well, then we just have to make a decision based on what he told you," Pam concluded.

"Heading into danger; it's not like we haven't done that enough since becoming Guardians," Cole snorted.

"Who are the Sleepers?" Tia questioned looking at Telara who shrugged. For some reason, she had not thought to ask Zach that question.

"Sounds like more enemies to me," Chance groaned leaning back in his chair, reminding Telara more of his brother.

"Sleepers aside, he told you if we go on this mission, we will find the town and free them, correct?" Pam asked.

"He also said she would lose something she never knew she had," I.Q. said looking thoughtful. "The question is what is it?"

"He also said that doing this could change your destiny," Pam informed him. "Maybe you will be able to defeat the Magine without any sacrifices."

"Is that worth losing something that we don't know about?" Chance asked. "Without knowing what that something is can we chance it? What if that something is what is meant to help us defeat the Magine?"

"What if what we find in this village not only helps us to defeat the Magine but also helps us do it without any casualties?" Pam countered. She looked over at Telara. "But the decision is yours to make; where you lead, we will follow."

"Great, so I get to decide between two possible outcomes. Either one could be beneficial or catastrophic." Telara felt as if she was getting sick to her stomach. She pushed her tray of food away from her; she was no longer hungry. "I didn't ask for this; I never wanted to lead or make decisions such as this. My biggest worry should be whether or not my shoes are gonna clash with my outfit." Telara fought back the tears that was threatening to overflow. "I don't have any leadership skills."

"I thought you did pretty well during that last fight with the Shadows," Vanna murmured while the others nodded.

"Actually, that was a team effort," Telara pointed out. "We all made our own decisions then, and I think we should be able to now. I don't want anyone that is uncomfortable going to be forced to." She stood up and gave a sad smile. "If I don't go, knowing that I could be of some help to those unfortunate people, I will never be able to look myself in the mirror again. I'm going, but anyone who is uncomfortable going can stay behind and help cover our tracks. I'm not ordering anyone to go."

With that, she turned around and walked into Zeke's office.

Almost immediately, she heard the door open behind her and saw them all walk in.

Cole gave her a smile. "You actually think we are gonna let you play the hero without us there?" Telara gave him a grateful smile.

"We started this together, and we will finish this together," Tia told her with a smile. "After all, Zach is only a male; he can't always be right."

That brought a chuckle from the girls and a glare from the guys. Tia with her feminist remarks. Telara couldn't imagine going through this without her; they had been together since birth, having been born on the same date and time, and they had always planned to grow old together. She looked around the room realizing they had all planned the same thing; she remembered the cracks they had always made about being in the old folks home with Cole and Chad chasing nurses in their walkers and wheelchairs. Would they come true now?

She couldn't do this without any of them. Without I.Q. and his smarts, they would be blind; Vanna was the glue that held them all together; Chance was always one to stand up for his friends; Cole and Chad were the comic relief; Tia kept them all focused; and Pam was more of a leader than Telara could ever think of being. Besides that, everyone here was her friend.

"You guys ready?" Zeke asked.

"As ready as we will ever be," Telara told him.

They grabbed the utility belts that would carry all the extra crystals they would be using. Illusion, or glamour crystals as they were now called, were hanging from the belts. They might need some kind of glamour to hide from mortals in case they accidentally stumbled upon any. Pam had a few of the healing Crims along with the memory Crims. Since they had never been properly trained to use them, it was a unanimous decision that Pam be in charge of them.

They stepped into the transporter and put on their sunglasses. Tia reached over and squeezed Telara's hands in reassurance. Telara squeezed back in thanks.

TELARA LOOKED AROUND NAMELESS ISLE AND COULD SEE nothing but trees and vegetation as far as she could see. They had been walking for several minutes and still she saw no water. How anyone could not see an island this huge was beyond her but, then again, Sanctuary was hidden from prying eyes, and that was larger than their hometown and at least several of the surrounding cities. In addition, they had said this place was hidden by magic so old that no one knew who had hidden this island from mortals.

"Report Alpha Leader."

They could hear Claw's Scottish drawl in their heads and saw the tightening of Pam's jaw. Even though they were all working together now, and he was able to create all the new techs with crystals, Claw still insisted on calling Pam "Alpha Leader." Telara suspected it had more to do with the fact that he enjoyed irritating her than actually trying to be cruel, but she had no plans on telling that to Pam.

Pam responded in a tight voice, "No visual as of yet, Claw, unless you count the occasional bird flying by."

"All right. Zeke told me to tell ye that Ira has been asking fer ye guys."

"In other words, hurry up and get back," Pam said dryly.

Claw chuckled. "Pretty much. Be careful out there."

"Awwww the mighty Scotsman is worried about us," Telara simpered with a smile.

They heard a grunt.

"I just don't feel like having to fill out all the paperwork that is required when a mission goes awry," Claw enlightened them.

"Don't worry about us, Claw. Just keep up your job of keeping Ira clueless for a bit longer. We will let you know if we find anything," Pam assured him.

"Sure thing Alpha Leader." They could hear the grin in Claw's voice.

Almost an hour later and still no sight of any ancient village with, or even one without, people walking around. They saw no evidence that there was any life on this island at all. It looked as if they were the first people to ever step foot on this island. Finally, Chad plopped down on a boulder they found in a clearing.

"I think it is safe to assume this town doesn't exist, and it is just a bedtime story told in Sanctuary." He wiped off the sweat from his forehead then, with a grin, slung it towards his brother who gave him a dirty look.

"If it is a bedtime story told in Sanctuary how did the singer come across it?" Cole huffed.

"There are many Sanctuary residents who have decided to live with mortals rather than stay in Sanctuary with their families," Pam pointed out. "He could be the child of one them and just heard the story from them."

Cole took a deep breath and stared up into the sky with a very dejected look on his face. They all knew how much he wanted this to be true, and they couldn't even take a poke at him for it. They all felt a bit frustrated at not locating this town; the thought that someone out there might know more about the Shadows and possibly a way to defeat the Magine without them losing their lives was very tantalizing. The symbols that Pam saw gave them hope (at least, that was the reason for that thinking) but what if they were just artistic and meant nothing?

Telara sighed, trying not to let the gloomy feelings get to her, she really was trying to be more upbeat, but now they had to return to Sanctuary with no more information than they had started out with.

Maybe Zach will be able to tell me something.

A noise to her right interrupted her thoughts. When she turned around, she saw a pair of green eyes staring out of the bushes at her.

"Ummm…guys," she said softly, hoping not to startle the pair of eyes watching them with curiosity. When they didn't pause in their heated discussion, she decided to get their attention with a very loud mind shout.

"Guys!"

They all stopped and, after noticing her staring into the bushes, they turned their attentions there. Green Eyes realized he had all their attention and took off running down a path they had not noticed being there before. It was a boy who could not be older than nine or ten. They all took off trying to catch the boy, but he was too fast for them.

At the end of the path, they were stunned to see the exact village that was on the screen during the concert right there in front of them. They looked around but could no longer see the boy they had been following. Not sure exactly how to proceed, they walked down the dirt lane trying to dodge the chickens that were scurrying around the road. Cole got into a fight with a goat who took a liking to Cole's shirt and was proceeding to make a lunch out of it.

"Hey! Get off me!" Cole was yanking his shirt out of the goat's mouth.

R-i-i-i-p-p-p!

"Awwww, man! My mom is so going to kill me," he groaned looking down at his torn shirt.

Chad was chuckling over his friend's plight. "Goat: 1, Cole: 0." Chad help up one finger with his left hand then with his right formed a circle. Cole just glared at him.

"You are not from around here, are you?" a soft voice said from their right.

When they turned around, they all got a shock. There standing in front of them was the blond-haired girl from the video in a light blue dress with a white smock and many multi-colored scarves wrapped around her hair and neck. Many bright colored beads adorned her wrists and neck.

"Ummmmm…what gave you that idea?" Chad stuttered.

She raised her eyebrows before gesturing towards their ensemble. "I have never seen any outfits such as yours."

They looked down at their jeans, sneakers, and cotton shirts. They looked at each other, not exactly sure how to handle this situation. The only one who had honestly expected to find the village was Cole and even he looked lost for words. Pam was the first to recover.

"No, we are from a village off the mainland," she was quick to say.

The girl gave them very appraising looks as if she could see right through the lie. "Which village would that be?"

"Dragoon," Cole said before Pam could answer. Telara groaned inside, sure there was no Dragoon village in ancient Greece.

The girl smiled at them. "Well, welcome to Lapros friends from Dragoon." They all tried to hide their expressions of shock that she had actually believed Cole. "I will advise you to be careful around here; many do not trust outsiders." She gave them a tentative smile before leaving them standing there.

"Ummm…okay." Chad looked to Pam. "So, what do we do now?"

"We free the town," Cole said with a smile.

"And exactly how do we do that?" I.Q. asked.

Cole looked over at I.Q. with a cocky grin. "You are the brains of this here outfit; you tell us. Doesn't that purple box you got say anything about the town of Lapros?"

"This is actually a village and not a town," I.Q. told him. "It would take more than what you see here for this place to qualify as a town."

Cole rolled his eyes. "Okay get technical on me why don't you," he grunted.

I.Q. just shrugged his shoulders, sat down on a nearby boulder, took out the Stargazer, and rapidly began tapping keys. "The first thing we need to figure out is how this village became cursed." More tapping. "It says here that Lapros was the home of one of the Paladins."

"Paladins?" Tia queried.

"Do you want to know what it says about this village or not?" I.Q. stared at Tia who clamped her lips shut and made a zipping gesture with her fingers. "It says here that the Paladin decided to take residence here when he fell in love with a local seamstress. It also says that the seamstress gave birth to twin boys."

"What else?" Cole peered with frustration over I.Q.'s shoulder to watch the colored symbols floating on the screen. The fact that I.Q. was the only one who could read the symbols was very confusing, even to I.Q., who could still not explain why it was that way.

"That is it." I.Q. was tapping on the keys, watching the screen, and reading the symbols.

"No reason why the town disappeared?" Pam asked, her forehead crinkling a bit.

I.Q. shook his head.

"Where did the Paladin go after the town disappeared?" Cole asked.

I.Q. shrugged his shoulders. "It does not say. As a matter of fact, I cannot find another reference in here about Lapros or thePaladin ."

"Well, that is a lot of help," Chad grumbled. "Ouch!" He glared at Vanna who had just elbowed him. "What was that for?"

"Can you be anymore insensitive?" She glared at him.

"Sure," Chad told her dodging the second elbow.

"Looks like this is a mystery we are going to have to solve on our own." Telara smiled at them. "Just call us 'Mystery Inc.'"

"Mystery Inc.?" Pam looked at her strangely.

Telara shook her head with a laugh. Pam fit in so well with them that sometimes it was easy to forget that she grew up in

Sanctuary and her experiences with what they considered everyday experiences were completely different. "Remind me when we get home, and I will show you what I mean." Pam still looked confused but nodded. "Okay team, time to solve this mystery! So where do we start first?"

I.Q. looked towards the town and nodded in that direction. "I guess a tour of the town might be in order." He looked down at his clothes and added, "But I think a change in wardrobe is needed first."

10

Before they could find themselves clothes, they were confronted by a very rotund, balding man who smiled as his voice boomed around them.

"The Guardians!"

They each wore an identical expression of pure confusion, standing in the middle of this town that looked as if it came off the pages of a history book while the portly fellow greeted them like old friends. They looked at each other before turning back to look at him.

"Do we know you?" Pam asked.

He looked her over, his brow creasing. "I thought there were only seven Guardians."

"I'm not a Guardian," Pam told him with one of those signature looks they remembered from their first meeting with her. Weird to see that look after all they had been through, although they were happy it wasn't directed at them.

The guy seemed to dismiss her from his thoughts and turned his attention to the others, as if the fact that she wasn't a Guardian meant she was of no importance. Telara had to admit that it irritated her. "The Guardians are a legend; we have been waiting for you to come to our aide for such a long time."

"What do you mean, waiting for us?" Cole asked moving from the back of the group forward.

The guy stared at Cole, making him feel very uncomfortable. This town was getting more and more confusing to them. This guy had seemed so happy to see them, but the look he gave Cole didn't feel as welcoming. But it was momentary as he smiled at them once again.

"Why, the story of the Guardians has been the only hope for everyone in this town."

Only hope? Great, that was all they needed. Not like they didn't have enough pressure back home where they were the only ones who could defeat the Magine. Now they were a town's only hope, a town they never knew existed before yesterday.

"Only hope for what?" Pam asked him, bringing his attention grudgingly back to her, something the others were thankful for. They hadn't even thought to ask that, so overwhelmed by them for being another's only hope.

"To free the town of course." He tried once again to dismiss Pam and turned to the others. "As I said, we have been waiting for so long."

"How long?" I.Q. asked him, adjusting his glasses.

"For longer than we can remember."

Well, if that wasn't cryptic…

"Who are you?" Pam asked him.

"I am the Archon of Lapros." If possible, the man's belly inflated more. "You may call me Myron."

"Archon?" Cole looked just as confused as the rest of them; well, all of them except Pam.

"An Archon is the leader of a town, kind of like a mayor," she explained to the group.

Myron nodded to her. "That is what I am." His voice was full of self-importance that could be heard clearly.

"How did you know that we are the Guardians?" Telara asked him, wondering exactly how many others knew about them that they knew nothing about. Back home, they were just regular teenagers who get dismissed easily, but everywhere else they went to they were almost revered. Which still weirded them out.

He looked at them standing there in their jeans, T-shirts, and sneakers.

Okay, maybe that had been a stupid question.

"Enough questions," Myron stated with a nod. "Follow me, and I will get you clothed and fed. You will stay in my home during your time with us."

They looked at each other, but they really didn't have a choice; they followed Myron back to his home. A home that put all the other little huts they had seen to shame. This was no hut. It was even bigger than their own homes, although nothing like what Raven or Vanna lived in. The walls were of stone while the furniture and other decorations inside spoke of great wealth. Tapestries hung from the walls, there were busts on pedestals, and was that fruit bowl made of real gold?

"Agathe!" he bellowed, and a very petite dark-haired woman appeared. She was wearing a light blue dress that draped over her shoulder. "Show our guests to their rooms."

She bowed to the man before turning to them and telling them to follow her.

THEIR ROOMS WERE GORGEOUS: WHITE STUCCO WALLS WITH arched windows and gold-colored draperies. Beds were rounded and large. In each of the beds, you could easily fit four people comfortably.

"Now I know what floating on a cloud feels like," Vanna murmured dreamily as she lay back on her bed. She wasn't wrong; the bed was soft.

They had just settled in when they were summoned for dinner with Archon Myron.

"Finally, some answers," Pam said,

They nodded in agreement. This house was gorgeous, in its Archaic way, but they were on a time limit and needed answers.

Every attempt to get their questions answered at dinner ended in their frustration and the Archon smiling at them. They would ask a question and suddenly find some type of delicious food practically shoved under their noses or a juggler would come in juggling fruit, cups, or whatever he could grab.

"Hey! Give that back!" The juggler had grabbed one of the extra crystals from Cole's belt. They laughed as it took Cole several minutes and a few crashes into the dinner table before he got it back. Myron roared with laughter.

Realizing he had pleased his employer, the juggler attempted to try another. Poor guy targeted Pam who stopped him with just a look. Another round of laughter followed as the juggler slunk away from her in defeat.

Myron stood up. "Thank you for such great entertainment, little juggler friend." The juggler bobbed his head as he disappeared through the arched doorway closing the drapes behind him. Myron turned to the others and gave a small nod of his head. "It is time for us to retire. We have had an eventful day and now we are all in need of some rest."

"But you haven't answered any of our questions!" Pam protested.

Myron looked her over, kind of like how you would look at a bug that was buzzing around you, driving you nuts, and you were thinking of a way to make it go away. Telara felt an unease in the bottom of her stomach; she had a feeling they weren't getting any questions answered tonight.

"They can wait until the morning; we have plenty of time."

That was it: they didn't have plenty of time. But no amount of protests from any of them would sway Myron as they found themselves ushered off to their prospective rooms.

"Claw is probably having a fit right now," Chance muttered as they followed Agathe to the wing where their rooms were. He grunted when he walked into Pam who had stopped right in front of him with no warning. "What gives?"

She turned to look at them. "We have been here for hours and not one word from Claw."

"Take it that's not normal?" Vanna asked her.

"On a mission, no."

They said nothing more until Agathe left them for the night, promising she would wake them for breakfast with the Archon. They walked into Pam's room where she attempted to contact Claw but got no response. Telara tried with the same result. As each one of them said Claw's name into their Crim with no response, it was becoming clear that they weren't going to be talking to the Gamma Leader anytime soon.

"Maybe some sleep, and we can try again tomorrow."

Telara nodded at I.Q.'s suggestion. She wasn't sure she was optimistic enough to believe they would be able to succeed tomorrow, but she was truly tired and just wanted some sleep.

"It would be better to have some more information before

contacting him," Pam agreed. "And come tomorrow, we will have more information one way or another."

The determination in her voice almost had Telara and the others feeling bad for Myron. Almost…

THE SOUND OF CLANGING HAD TELARA OPENING HER EYES. Looking around the room, she saw a very gorgeous, curly and blond-haired woman. The woman picked up a golden vase, examined it, wrinkled her nose, and tossed it on a small pile of other pieces on the floor that wasn't there when Telara had gone to sleep. Now, she knew what the noise was that had awakened her.

She tried clearing her throat to get the woman's attention but when that didn't work, she rose her voice. "Hey!"

The blond turned and smiled a very brilliant smile. "Finally, the sleeping mortal awakes."

Mortal? She watched as the woman flounced, yes flounced, to the bed before gracefully sitting down on it without disturbing anything. She didn't walk or stride over to the bed; she flounced, and her sheer pink gauzy dress flounced along with her. Telara was trying to think of who this woman reminded her of. After she sat down, barely making an impression on the bed, she looked at Telara as if waiting for her to say something. Telara just wasn't sure exactly what.

"Can I help you?" Telara finally asked after the silence was so quiet it was actually loud.

The woman on her bed fluffed her hair so that it bounced even more.

Fitting her and her flouncy ways, Telara thought.

When the woman spoke, her voice carried around the room

softly, almost melodically. Barbie! That was who this woman reminded her of. Not the girls at her school they called Barbie, but the actual dolls that looked so perfect. Not a hair out of place, and she was betting this woman had never had a zit in her life with her flawless skin.

"Actually mortal, I am here to help you."

Telara frowned. There goes that mortal thing again.

The woman tilted her head, looking at Telara as if she was an anomaly she couldn't understand. "You would think that a mortal such as you would know how to show a Goddess the proper enthusiasm." The woman smiled at the look on Telara's face. "Yes, this beautiful Goddess has taken time out of her busy schedule to come give aide to you poor mortals."

Telara knew she was staring, knew her eyes had to be the size of saucers, but seriously? A Goddess? She knew she was a descendant of some God or Goddess somewhere; she wouldn't have these neat powers if she wasn't. That didn't mean she ever expected to be talking to one. She pinched her arm to see if she was dreaming and looked back up. Nope, not a dream. Barbie Goddess was still sitting there. The woman frowned at her... er, the Goddess frowned at her.

"Goddess?"

The Goddess's smile grew with pride at the fact that Telara was sitting there staring at her in total shock. "Aphrodite to be exact."

That explained the whole Barbie image. "I thought you dealt with matters of the heart." Telara frowned at her. "This isn't a mission of the heart; we are trying to free this village from a curse. Isn't this something more up Athena's or Artemis's alley?"

Aphrodite's eyes flashed, and the whole room lit up in brilliant light; it was so bright that Telara had to cover her eyes.

When the light faded, there were spots before her eyes, and Aphrodite was gone.

"You never insult a God or Goddess if you want answers from them."

Telara looked at Pam with a frown. She had told her friends about the dream, but she didn't expect Pam's reaction. "How did I insult her?"

"Aphrodite, Athena, and Artemis have what you could call a rivalry going on."

"You talk as if you know them personally," Chad interrupted but pressed his lips together when Pam frowned at him.

"You can find that information in any history book," Pam said before continuing. "Athena and Artemis have always considered Aphrodite a bit of an airhead." She gave a shrug. "So, Aphrodite is always trying to prove that her power is just as valuable as theirs."

"Every God or Goddess has their own power that serves a purpose," Vanna protested. Vanna was their mother nature, who believed that everyone was equal and that no one was better than anyone else.

Pam just laughed. "Don't tell them that; they live to think they are better than the others."

"That is nice but just how did I insult her?" Telara interrupted feeling very irritated with everything.

"You basically told her that you wanted Athena's or Artemis's help and not hers."

Telara opened her mouth to deny it, but she knew Pam was right.

"Aphrodite is the Goddess of Love. What can she do to help us?" Cole asked. He immediately regretted asking that once Pam turned her gaze onto him. He started squirming under her stare.

"She is a Goddess," Pam told them simply. "Her powers aren't the only things that are valuable."

Telara's eyes widened as she realized her mistake: Aphrodite wasn't offering her powers; she was offering information. She groaned. "How was I to know? Not like I expected to come face-to-face with a God or Goddess."

Pam shrugged, and they all started to head down the stairs. "No sense dwelling on it; next time, remember to stroke the ego just a bit."

"Stroke the ego?" Telara followed and frowned.

"The only thing more powerful than their powers is their ego," Pam said as they walked past the foyer heading to the dining room. "You stroke their egos, say a few flattering things, and pray they give you something useful."

"But why is Aphrodite, the Goddess of Love, here?" Tia's forehead was furrowed.

Pam shrugged. "In some of the stories or myths, they told of how Aphrodite hated being looked at as a flighty Goddess with no real mettle to her. So, to get back at the other Gods or Goddesses who treated her as a…" Pam paused as if trying to come up with the right word.

"Ditz?" Cole supplied, and Pam nodded.

"A ditz. Aphrodite would involve herself in the affairs of the other Gods and Goddesses to sabotage their plans."

"You saying this town is the result of a God or Goddess?" Telara wasn't sure she liked the sound of that.

Cole stopped, and his mouth hung open. This caused Tia to

quip with a grin while walking past him, "Better close that fly trap."

"The song!" They all stopped and turned to look at Cole. "Those that walk among the clouds! The Gods!"

"Cole," Telara started, but he interrupted her.

"You can't call this a coincidence, Telly. No way," he protested, and she sighed.

"I don't know what I am calling this. All I know is we need hardcore answers, no more guessing."

They entered the dining area where one of the servants was walking out, leaving a very irritated looking Pam standing next to the table that was laden down with all kinds of food. The boys, including I.Q., all took a seat and started filling their plates, stuffing bacon or sausage into their mouths as they did. Pam looked at Telara with a wry look on her face.

"It would have been nice if Aphrodite had told you something considering our host has decided to take leave this morning and leave us on our own."

They stared around the room realizing that Myron was indeed a no show. If Telara didn't feel bad before, she sure did now.

"Not necessarily," I.Q. spoke up. "Who's to say her information would have even been helpful? I have read the myths and know that sometimes the Gods or Goddesses just love to mess with us mortals."

"Who's to say it wouldn't have been helpful?" Pam spoke with no censure but mere fact. Telara really wished the ground would just open up and swallow her whole right now.

Vanna walked over to the table and grabbed herself a roll. "So, no sense in crying over spilled ambrosia." They groaned at her pun; she had tried but fell just a bit flat. "I say we go and do some exploring and see what we find."

"Excellent idea."

They turned to see a very tall slender male with thinning hair smiling at them. His tunic practically dwarfed his body. He had to stand over 6 feet tall but looked as if one big gust of wind would have carried him off to Oz.

"The Archon has asked me to see to your needs as he has been called away for village business. So, I will play your guide for the day."

11

THEY FOLLOWED Mr. Beanpole around the town as he pointed out the marketplace, telling them which stall had the sweetest fruit and best prices. It was becoming quite a show watching Pam ask him questions about what was going on with the town and Mr. Beanpole pointing out where the best fabric is sold. Telara and Tia tried to hold back their smirks when they could hear Cole and Chad in their mental conversation taking bets on how long before Pam beans Mr. Beanpole over the head with the nearest clay pot.

Their tour got cut short when a pixie-like brown-haired girl ran up to Mr. Beanpole and whispered something in his ear. He turned to Telara and apologized, saying he was needed elsewhere. She nodded and looked at the others.

"Looks like we are on our own."

The boys gave an excited shout over that; they were growing bored following Mr. Beanpole around.

Pam looked over at them. "We still need answers."

Telara shrugged. "So, let's find some."

That was easier said than done; it seemed everyone they

tried talking to kept wanting to change the subject on them. Whenever they mentioned anything about a curse, the person would actually shut up shop and almost run away.

"Is this a conspiracy or what?" Chance stared at the fruit lady who had quickly turned away from them to help a guy who had suddenly appeared.

Pam gave a frustrated sigh. "Claw," she said out loud to see if they could get in contact with the Gamma captain. They had tried several times already but no response. Her brow furrowed. The others attempted to contact him as well, but each one got the same response.

"What do we do?"

Telara wasn't sure how to answer Tia; they had been here over twenty-four hours with no results. They didn't know anything more than they had yesterday.

"We leave."

They all turned to look at Pam not believing what they were hearing. Vanna spoke what was on their minds.

"But what about the people in this village? We just walk away and leave them to their fate?"

"If they wanted help, they should have thought of that before stonewalling us," Tia grumbled.

"Your parents are expecting you home tonight," Pam interjected as she saw Cole glare at Tia. She wanted to avoid another Tia/Cole spat.

They looked at each other as they realized it was Sunday; they had come to the island Saturday morning. Their parents were expecting them, but these islanders needed them. Pam wasn't done.

"If you don't get home, your parents will become suspicious and then we chance sabotaging everything."

"Yeah 'cause us training to die is more important than these poor people."

Pam's face went white at Cole's words. The others stared at him, their eyes wide and mouths open; he was the fun loving one, but you could hear the anger in his words.

"Cole, that isn't fair," Vanna told him softly.

"No, he is right," Telara said causing the others to look at her warily. "But it is also what we all agreed to this past summer and sniping at Pam about it doesn't change that."

Cole blanched from the censure in Telara's voice. She too hated the fact that they had to leave this village when they came here to help them; she also hated the fact that they were all training to die before they could even legally go to a bar. But the fact still remained that that is what they had to do. Tia was right; the people were stonewalling them at every turn. How do you help people who won't help themselves?

"Sorry, Pam," Cole said not looking at her.

"Come on, guys! We need to head out," Telara said not liking the tension she was feeling between everyone. "Maybe someone from Sanctuary can take our place until we are able to return." Vanna gave her a small smile, and they started to head out of the village.

The sun was getting low as they started the trek out of the village. To them, it felt as if they had been walking for hours and yet they still couldn't find the path that had brought them to the village only yesterday.

Cole and Chad both stopped and sat down on some tree stumps, looking around at the trees and grass. Every path they walked down took them back to the village. When they decided to walk off the path, they still didn't get too far. They were all tired, thirsty, and getting hungry.

"Exactly how big is this island?" Chance asked looking up and all around them.

Telara was standing next to Pam looking at the surrounding scenery.

"Do you even know where we are?" she asked as low as she could.

"About as much as you," was the reply.

"So, we have no idea what happened to this town or how to help them, and they won't help us."

It wasn't a question, and Pam didn't bother to answer the statement.

"Have you been able to contact Claw yet?" Telara asked. Pam shook her head.

"What was that?"

Telara turned to see the others looking to their left. Telara looked but saw only trees. She looked at Tia, but her eyes were looking above the trees. Pam gasped to her right. Turning quickly, her stomach dropped at what she saw. A dragon bigger than the trees that were towering over them landed on the ground in front of them. They all stumbled back, eyes wide, watching the beast before them as it spread its wings that had to be at least twelve feet long. The scales looked as if they were made of hot lava: they were bright red and looked as if they were moving. The tail looked longer than the wings. It swayed back and forth with spikes sticking up and glowing as red as the scales on its body. The claws on its front paws looked as if they could shred rocks with just one swipe. From the nostrils, tendrils of steam flowed out as the dragon stared at them.

"Oh, the Gods!" Vanna gasped out. They really had been around their friends from Sanctuary way too much. Telara instantly noticed what had her friend astonished. The dragon's eyes changed from blood red to bright blue, almost human, before changing back once again to blood red.

The dragon leaned forward, his neck bending to stare at each of them. For some reason, Telara felt as if this dragon was telling them that they needed to turn back, that they weren't allowed to go any further. She felt her friends' agreement in that consensus through their mind link.

"Listen dragon … s-s-sir. We need to leave here. We do not belong in this village; we need to go home," Telara implored.

Telara was seriously thinking that it was time for a change in leadership; she was so not ready to be talking to a fire breathing dragon. She could feel the eyes of her friends on her, could hear their thoughts of thinking she was crazy through their mind link.

They were probably right, she thought as she held her breath and waited for the dragon to burn them all to a crisp.

"Gee, sorry mom. Can't make family night this month. I got invited to a barbecue with a dragon." Her nervousness was showing as she cracked jokes about their impending deaths.

The other Guardians heard her, though; none could keep their thoughts from the others. Cole snickered, but Vanna gave Telara a dirty look.

"Is now the time for a sense of humor?" she demanded.

Telara shrugged her shoulders. Pam gave them a questioning look to which Telara just tapped her forehead. Pam just shook her head.

"So, boss lady, got any ideas on what to do now?" asked Chad.

"Pray?" Telara suggested, her voice tight with tension. Of course, she was tense; who wouldn't be tense with a big red dragon staring down at them? Although she was sure if the dragon wanted to charbroil them or eat them, it would have done so already.

"Maybe he is deciding if we would taste better with ketchup or not," Cole thought with a smirk, and Vanna threw up her hands in frustration.

Tia just smacked him upside his head. *"Way to go, Cole; just give him some ideas why don't you?"*

Big mistake. The dragon turned to look at Cole and Tia. Everyone held their breath. The dragon moved its snout closer to Cole and sniffed him, causing him to stumble back with a yelp and fall over a tree root.

"Cole, your crim!" Pam shouted out.

The Dragon's red spiky ears, or what they assumed were his ears, seemed to twitch, but his eyes stayed on Cole.

Cole grabbed his flame crystal that was hanging around his neck and yanked it off. However, instead of the fiery numchuks they were expecting, his flame crystal dangled there from the metal chain looking very non-threatening. He looked at the others who were all staring at his flame crystal with the same look of apprehension on their faces. The others tried to get their Crims to work as well, but Vanna's belt just dangled from her hands, Tia's bands stayed put as did I.Q.'s watch, Chad's ring, and Chance's earring. Telara attempted to get her Rotary to do anything, but it just glinted off the setting sun.

They were in serious trouble.

"Nooooo! Stop!!!"

They turned and saw the blond with the scarves and bangles again. They looked at each other then back at the woman who was standing between them and the dragon.

"You have to let them pass, please. They don't belong here."

They couldn't decide if she was the bravest or most stupid

person they had met, but she did distract the dragon from Cole. It turned its gaze onto her and steam wafted around her.

"Who the hell is she?" Cole stared at the crazy lady who didn't seem scared that she was standing in front of a fire breathing monster who could have her for lunch.

Telara was slowly shaking her head, not sure exactly what to do. She wasn't trained for this. Their Crims didn't work, they couldn't reach out to Claw, and some lady who wasn't even from their time zone was trying to protect them from a dragon.

"Whoever she is, she got some balls." They could hear the admiration in Chance's voice and had to agree with that.

"Guys!" They looked over at Pam who was looking at them, pointing at herself. "Person with no mental issues here. I don't know what you guys are saying to each other, but I am getting really nervous here and would like in on the conversation. Without our Crims, we are sitting ducks."

"Right!" Telara nodded feeling contrite about them excluding Pam from their conversation, although their mind speak had become second nature to them. "Sorry."

"Go!" The blond told them, but they stared at her.

"We can't leave you here," Cole protested.

"He won't hurt me," she promised, and they noticed the dragon just stared at the blond in front of him.

"I think we should listen…"

"Cole!" Vanna spoke out loud, reminding him that Pam couldn't hear their mind speak.

Cole gave a contrite look before speaking so Pam could hear this time. "I think we should listen to her." When the others went to protest, he pointed to the dragon who was just watching them. "Look at him. If he was going to hurt her, he would have done it already."

"Well, here goes nothing then." Telara decided to be the first to move past the dragon. She started walking, keeping her eyes on the dragon and the woman who was standing in front of him trying to keep his attention on her. She had just begun to walk past the dragon when its tail landed in front of her with a great Whoomph! The force of the impact threw Telara back the four steps she had taken, landing her on her butt in the dirt.

"Ummpph!" Telara stood up, brushing off the dirt and leaves and glaring up at the dragon who just stared at her with its red glowing eyes.

"No!" the woman yelled at the dragon.

"He doesn't seem to want to hurt us," Vanna said then gave a chuckle when Telara gave her a pointed look. "You are still alive, aren't you?"

Telara gave a humph.

"But I get the feeling he will not let us pass," Pam noted.

"Ya think?" Telara didn't mean to sound so sarcastic, but her posterior was still feeling bruised.

"Apparently more than you," Pam pointed out.

"Hey, I thought about it," Telara protested.

"As you were doing it," Pam said with a grin which caused the others to just stare at her. They were standing there with a dragon right in front of them, and she cracks a joke.

"So, give us your big plan then," Telara retorted.

"We go back to the village."

"And our parents?"

Pam looked at the dragon then back at Telara. "And if we keep trying to pass by the dragon, we may end up with more than just a bruised ego."

Pam started to move slowly away from the dragon with the

others following suit. That was when they noticed that the woman was now gone. Where did she go?

Cole looked at Tia who looked at Telara. They needed to find that woman; she might have the answers to their questions.

"I think we need to regroup and try to come up with a better solution than just walking out of here. We need a plan." Telara nodded to Pam as the others started to follow Pam's lead and slowly back away from the dragon till it was just Telara standing there glaring at the dragon who was watching her, as if daring her to try it again.

"Telly."

Telara nodded at Vanna, giving the dragon one last look. "I will be back big boy, and I will be leaving this town, and you will not be stopping me."

The dragon inclined his head towards her as if to say you are more than welcome to try. Telara just glared and turned around, walking back to the village.

"You just turned your back on the dragon?" Pam looked at her as if she thought she was crazy, and they all headed back to town.

Telara shrugged. "It seems as long as we are doing what he wants to do we are safe. I just wasn't walking away without giving him a piece of my mind."

"You really need to work on that temper girl," Pam told her. "I think your friends would like to have you around for their final battle with the Magine."

12

____

"WHAT IS that Disney movie called again? Oh, that is right: *Sleeping Beauty.*" Telara could hear the softly spoken voice, so familiar.

"How did they wake her up again?" the voice murmured as if the person was talking to themselves trying to solve a problem. Telara tried to open her eyes. After they had gotten back to the village, Archon Myron had asked about their whereabouts.

"Oh, that is right. She was woken up by true love's kiss." Still that voice spoke.

Telara felt the weight of sleep keeping her eyes closed, as if Hypnos himself was keeping her asleep. When they had confronted Myron about the dragon, he had told them that the dragon cursed the town and that as long as the dragon lived, the town would always be cursed. They told him that it would have been nice to know this before they had met the beast.

Myron had spoken of how easy they could kill the dragon and free the town. They had just stared at him. Their Crims didn't work here, and they weren't even sure if the Crims could even kill the dragon. He didn't look like a Shadow Creature. Cole had spoken via their mind speak to say that he didn't feel right with what Myron was saying; he got a totally different feeling from the dragon.

They had all fallen into bed exhausted and now there was a voice close to her ear interrupting Telara's sleep.

"Well, I am the Goddess of Love, am I not?" Telara's eyes jerked open, and she stared into the blue eyes of a smiling Aphrodite. "Aha, sleeping beauty awakes."

Telara jerked up in bed, looking around her then back at Aphrodite. "Am I sleeping?"

Aphrodite laughed. "Olympus, no! Can't have Morpheus listening in now, can we? You are very much awake." She walked around the room, her fingers absently running over furniture and the draperies.

Telara got out of bed and turned to face Aphrodite who was smiling at her. She wasn't sure exactly what to say; she didn't want to offend her and have her disappear on her again.

"Well, hello Aphrodite. Although you are a bit late; Myron told us last night that the dragon had cursed the town. Unless you want to tell us how to get rid of the dragon..." Telara looked at her and, to her amazement, Aphrodite laughed.

"And you believed the pot-bellied male?"

Telara frowned. "You are saying he lied to us?"

"I am saying that Myron, like anyone in power who wants to keep that power, will say anything or do anything to further their own agenda."

Telara licked her lips. "So, will killing the dragon end this curse?"

Aphrodite turned and smiled at her. "What do you think?"

Telara groaned. Just what she needed. "I don't know. That is why I am asking you."

A petite blond brow raised. "If you are going to get testy with me, I will just leave."

Telara sighed and swallowed her irritation. "Sorry," she said between clenched teeth. "Just no one wants to give us answers, and the dragon won't let us leave the village."

"Of course, he won't." She smiled, and Telara wanted to scream.

"Why, though, if he isn't the reason for this curse?"

"I never said he wasn't the reason for the curse." Aphrodite smiled. "Be careful who you trust; those that smile at you aren't always your friend."

"You are talking in riddles."

"Then let me clear this up for you little mortal." Aphrodite appeared right in front of her. "You have woken up a Goddess that will not want you to leave this town."

Telara bit back a retort about personal space; she was more curious about what Aphrodite had just revealed. "Why?"

The Goddess smiled. "Simple. If you are in this town when it disappears, you will disappear along with it."

"But if we were to disappear with the town, we wouldn't be able to defeat the Magine," Telara protested. "I thought the Gods and Goddesses needed us for that."

Aphrodite smiled sweetly at her. "I guess you would be thinking that."

Telara tried not to get frustrated and snap at her; she tried remembering what Pam had told her. To get information, you needed to stroke their egos. Then again, the only information she was getting was more riddles.

"Well, we are trying to rid the world of the darkness for the Gods and Goddesses, aren't we?"

Aphrodite looked at her and smiled. Telara groaned, expecting more riddles.

"Let's just say that the Guardians are the Caretakers' best kept secret, until now."

Telara frowned at Aphrodite. "Until now? What makes us different, and why are we a secret from the Gods and Goddesses?"

"You seven are unlike the other Guardians."

Telara wanted to ask more questions about what made them different, but there was an even more pressing question that she truly needed answers to. So, for now, she would put the others on hold.

"So, how can we leave?"

"Isn't it obvious? You break the curse."

"How?"

"I can't do everything for you." Aphrodite gave her a patronizing smile. "You'll have to do some of the work on your own."

With that, Aphrodite started to fade away.

"Wait!" Telara hollered. "Why does this Goddess want us stuck here?"

Aphrodite smiled. "If you get out of this maybe I will tell you."

With that, she disappeared. Telara threw a pillow at the spot where the Goddess had stood only moments before, frustrated.

"Man, you get all the interesting dreams," Chance grumbled the following morning after she told them what had happened.

Telara just stared at him. "I tell you a Goddess wants us to be stuck in this town forever, and that is all you have to say?"

Chad chuckled. "You have to admit that you do get the most interesting people in your dreams."

"This wasn't even a dream!" Telara protested. The guys shrugged and she practically growled. "You know what? You guys can have Aphrodite anytime you want." Cold and Chance hi-fived each other while the girls just rolled their eyes at them.

"What we do know is that we can't trust Myron." Vanna got the conversation steered back to Telara's encounter with Aphrodite.

"Aphrodite made it sound like we can't trust anyone who has acted like our friends," Telara groused. Ever since that conversation, she has been up in her bedroom not able to go back to sleep. They didn't know how to get out of this village and if they didn't get out, they would never leave. They had to break this curse, and they have no idea how.

"So, let's find someone who hasn't been feeding us compliments." Tia grinned.

"And who would that be?" Telara asked her not moving.

"Blondie." They looked at each other as if they couldn't believe they hadn't thought about that. The blond who was in the video that they had met on their first day and who had stood up to the dragon. She was all the same person.

"How are we going to find her?" Cole asked. "We don't know where she is."

"This town can't be that big, can it?" I.Q. said with a shrug, and they all departed to find their blond would-be savior from the night before.

It was lunch time with their stomachs reminded them of

that fact and still there was no sight of the woman they were searching for. They hadn't wanted to go back to the Anarch's home; after Telara's chat with Aphrodite, they were very suspicious of him and his motives.

"We have searched this whole village and nothing." Tia leaned against one of the many wooden fences they had been walking around trying to find the woman from last night. In the center of town, there were markets selling everything that you would ever need; when you got out of the "city" part of town, there were wooden fences everywhere. Chickens and pigs ran through the main part and the exterior part. To them, it seemed like chaos; yet, as Pam pointed out to them, back then this was considered normal.

They had walked around the center of town where the marketplace was located. Now, they were standing on a dirt path outside of the town where the small farms were situated. Telara looked over at Cole who was staring down at his broken necklace, testament that their Crims didn't work here. I.Q. reasoned that since they were stuck in a town that was in a time loop, maybe the Crims didn't exist in this time. Pam seemed to agree with him.

Pam, who seemed to feel just as bad about Cole's necklace as Telara, spoke up. "We can have Claw fix that when we get home."

"If we get home," Chad muttered kicking a stone and watching it skip down the dusty road.

"Don't say that Chad," Vanna protested. "We will get home; we just need faith."

"Faith is about as broken as this necklace," Cole said, his voice strained. He picked up a rock and, with a flick of his wrist, he sent the rock flying. They watched as it bounced off a boulder and went soaring into some nearby bushes.

"Ouch!"

They jerked around and saw the green-eyed boy they had first seen when they came to this island staring at them.

"It's green eyes!" Chad exclaimed, and the boy frowned at him.

"My name is Spiro!" the boy spat glaring at Chad.

"Spiro? As in the purple dragon?" Cole asked.

The boy looked at Cole. "You have a dragon, too?"

Chad snorted. "Yeah, kid, we got a dragon. Pixelated but still a dragon." He grinned.

Spiro frowned at them. "What does pixelated mean?"

Vanna kicked Chad who glared at her. She ignored his glare and knelt down by Spiro.

"Hello, Spiro. My name is Vanna. No, the dragon they are talking about is nothing like the one terrorizing your town."

Rather than clear things up for the little boy, he looked more confused. "Our dragon isn't terrorizing our town," he protested looking at them. "He is the one who has been wronged; he is a good dragon."

Cole snorted, and Tia elbowed him hard. "What?" He looked at her. "Good dragons don't stop people from leaving."

"It isn't his fault!" Spiro glared at Cole; his hands clenched into little fists by his side.

Cole put up his hands in surrender. "Okay, okay, little guy. Not his fault. Got it." The look on Cole's face clearly suggested he thought the boy had lost his mind. Telara was almost inclined to agree with Cole on this one. Who would defend a dragon that was keeping their town captive? Then Aphrodite's words came back to her, especially how she wouldn't give a straight answer about the dragon. Seemed there was much more to this story.

Just then, Telara's stomach growled and Tia's answered hers causing them all to laugh. Even Spiro laughed.

"Come with me. My sister makes the best stew in all the lands. She will feed you and tell you all about the dragon." He gave a proud grin. "She knows everything about the dragon." He motioned for them to follow him, and they took off.

"SPIRO, WHERE HAVE YOU BEEN? LUNCH HAS BEEN READY FOR A while now." They all stared at the blond who turned and, upon seeing them, they could see the surprise in her eyes.

"Safron, they were standing along the road to town when I found them. They said they have a dragon, too; a purple one! I told them our dragon was a good dragon, but I don't think they believe me. You have to tell them our dragon is a good one." Spiro's words were coming out so fast they weren't sure how his sister understood him, but she did. She smiled down at him.

"Go wash your hands, Spiro. We can tell them about the dragon after we all eat."

When Spiro opened his mouth to say something else, Cole's stomach growled. Spiro laughed and ran to wash his hands. She turned to them and smiled.

"My name is Safron. I am sure you have many questions, but your stomachs seem to be in need of some nourishment, so the answers can wait."

13
____

THEY ALL AGREED that Safron's stew was one of the best they had eaten, although they also agreed not to tell their mothers that. They helped her to clean up before everyone retired to the backyard where Spiro was playing with a brown puppy. They all looked at each other not sure how to start the conversation.

"So, I am sure you have some questions." Safron broke the silence.

"That is an understatement," Chad said, and Vanna shushed him.

Safron smiled at them. "That is all right; I understand."

Telara decided since Safron had broken the ice she was going to dive in. "Myron told us it was the dragon who had cursed this town and to break the curse we have to kill the dragon. But... someone else told me that Myron isn't to be trusted." She didn't feel comfortable telling Safron that the person that she had been talking with was a Goddess. Her friends were one thing, but this person she barely knew.

"That person is very wise," Safron told her, catching everyone's attention at that. Seemed their blond friend didn't think much of the Archon. "Myron has his own agenda."

"What do you mean?" I.Q. leaned forward watching Safron; you could already see the wheels turning in his head.

Safron took a deep breath and looked at them. "To explain that I would have to tell you the whole story of how Lapros got cursed, but it is a long one."

"Finally!" Tia sounded as exasperated as they all felt.

Telara tried not to laugh at Safron who was staring at Tia. It seemed Tia had startled her by her outburst.

"We have been asking that question since day one. No one has wanted to answer us," Telara explained to Safron.

Safron frowned then gave a rueful shake of her head. "Myron has the whole town too scared to say anything other than what he tells them to."

"But why?" Vanna asked.

Safron smiled at her. "As I said, this is a long story."

Cole shrugged. "We don't have anywhere to be."

"Okay." She smiled at them. "I am not sure how long ago this happened; time has come to have no meaning to any of us here in Lapros." They all nodded in understanding. "Long ago, strangers came to Greece, strangers with the powers of Gods. No one knew where they came from or even why they came to Greece."

She looked out to the west with a soft smile that held a lot of feeling. They looked but saw nothing but trees and some mountains even further. Looking back, she grinned at them and continued.

"They were different than any of the Gods or Goddesses that ruled Greece. They were kind and caring."

They looked at each other with the same look of disbelief

on their faces. Gods? Kind? Not any of the Greek ones that they knew of. They all had their own agendas.

Safron grinned and nodded at their expressions. "They not only mingled with the mere mortals of Greece, they lived among us as well instead of living up with the Gods and Goddesses of Olympus."

Safron laughed at their amazed expressions. "Yes, it was a sight to see. These strangers refused for us to treat them like Gods. No temples, no sacrifices, no offerings. To us mortals, it was like a dream come true; the strangers lived amongst us mortals, helped everyone, and asked for nothing in return."

They weren't sure why she seemed so saddened when she said that; it sounded pretty nice to them. Gods that were kind compared to those that were petty and cruel? They knew who they would choose.

"Then a darkness came to the land," she continued and gave a shiver at the memory.

"The Shadows?" Pam, who had been quiet, spoke up.

Safron frowned. "Shadows?"

"The creatures, the darkness you spoke of."

Safron shook her head looking confused. "I don't know about any creatures; all I remember is a darkness that threatened to swallow all the lands. I'm sorry I can't tell you more about the darkness. We never saw it; we had only heard stories, but they were enough to scare us all."

They looked at each other but said nothing, so Safron continued. "When the darkness came to the land, our people prayed to the Gods and Goddesses, but they turned their backs on us and left us to defend ourselves."

Telara saw I.Q. playing with the small compact Stargazer absently as he listened to Safron; she was sure when they got back to the Archon's tonight, he would be up tapping on it.

"So, when the Gods turned their back on us, it was the strangers who had chosen to live amongst us with the powers of Gods that came to our aid."

"What did they do?" Cole asked.

"They banished the darkness," Safron acknowledged with a nod. "I don't know how they did it, but they did, and they saved us all."

"That is good, right?" Chad asked as she had paused and seemed to be staring off into nothingness.

Safron didn't move, still staring into nothingness she spoke. Her voice had a faraway sound that resembled the look in her eyes. She was speaking of past events as if she were seeing them right in front of her eyes; Telara was sure she probably was.

"After the battle, the strangers left Lapros refusing any payment. They claimed none was needed. All but one of the strangers left; he settled down in Lapros; he was very kind and generous to all."

Telara looked at Tia, and they both heard the feeling beneath Safron's words. There was something there.

"The villagers welcomed him like a hero; they wanted to erect temples and statues in his honor, but he declined. He refused to be treated as a God, said he wasn't any better than the villagers."

There was a sadness to her voice. Even the air around them had a depressing aura.

"The Gods couldn't have been too happy about that," Pam spoke. It wasn't a question; it was a statement.

Safron shook her head, her eyes sparkling with unshed tears. There was something more to this story; there had to be with the sadness they could hear and feel coming off her. They didn't think this story was going to have a happy ending.

"Were you and he…involved?" Tia asked.

Safron nodded and gave a sad smile. "We were married and had twins." She shook her head when they looked at Spiro. "Spiro is my brother; our babies weren't here when Lapros and the stranger were cursed."

"*Twins.*" They looked at Vanna who was nodding towards the disk in I.Q.'s hands. "*Didn't the Stargazer speak of twins being born to a Paladin and the local seamstress?*"

She was right; they looked at each other then back at Safron with all her colorful scarves. She had to be the seamstress from the Stargazer, and that meant the stranger she was talking about would be the Paladin.

"Who cursed the town?" Telara asked, wanting to move past the conversation. She couldn't imagine what Safron was going through. Living all this time and not knowing what happened with your child had to be a mother's worst nightmare.

"Eris."

"Eris?" Chad chewed his lip.

"The Goddess of Discord, Strife, Tension, and pretty much anything that throws a monkey wrench into your day," Vanna grumbled.

"Monkey wrench?" Safron asked, looking confused.

"It is a saying from where we come from, meaning she likes to cause problems," Tia explained.

"Ohhh." Safron nodded. "That pretty much describes Eris."

"I thought her name was Discord," Chad asked then ducked as Vanna swatted at him telling him to shush.

"But she is just a minor Goddess," Chance protested. "Why would she be upset about the villagers wanting to worship this stranger?"

"Lapros worshiped Eris before the strangers came to the village."

Telara saw Pam's brow crease at Safron's words but since she couldn't read Pam's mind, that she knew of and neither was she inclined to try, she could only guess as to why.

"Eris' temple resides on the outskirts of town. During that time, it had become empty but now Myron makes sure that there are offerings daily to her."

"Wait! I thought that Gods and Goddesses were worshiped because of villages wanting a good crop season, victory in war, or something like that. Eris is the Goddess of Chaos," Cole chimed in and honestly Telara was curious about that question as well.

It was I.Q. who answered. "Eris is a known companion of Ares; I think the teacher even called her the Nurse of War once. I am sure if there was a town that she favored they would also find favor with Ares."

"Eris the Goddess of Discord and Strife was also called the Nurse of War?" They all nodded at Cole's incredulous question. Discord surely didn't sound like any attribute they would associate with a nurse.

Safron nodded at I.Q. much to everyone's disbelief. "Yes, Eris has been called the Nurse of War. She helps Ares to accomplish his bloody work. She enjoys the groans of the dying men on the battlefield, especially after she fills their hearts with hatred and encouraging the bloody battle all in the name of Ares."

They all gave a shudder at that thought.

"Does this town really look like a military town?" Chance asked. "All we have seen are merchants, servants, and politicians." He gave Safron an apologetic look. "Sorry, not meaning to be disrespectful."

She gave a shake of her head. "No apologies needed; our warriors were gone to war when the curse was placed on Lapros."

Tia snorted. "Ares probably didn't want to lose any precious warriors." The others nodded in agreement.

"So then Eris wasn't the only one who was behind Lapros being cursed?" Cole looked at Safron who nodded.

"It is believed that Eris went to Ares who cursed the stranger and changed him into a dragon, taking away Lapros's protection and letting Eris curse the town to never go forward. The town is always stuck in the time where we betrayed Eris so that we can never forget."

They looked at each other. The dragon that wouldn't let them leave was the Paladin the Stargazer had mentioned. From what Safron said, there were more than just one. Telara could see the gears turning in I.Q.'s mind. She was sure everyone's minds were churning over this new information as well.

"And Myron is attempting to get back into her favor," Pam stated, pulling them out of their reverie. Safron nodded. "So, back to him telling us to break this curse we need to kill the dragon," she prompted. "You said that he said that because he has his own agenda."

"I'm not sure why he would tell you that; I don't know if he has struck a bargain with the Goddess but what I do know is that every time the village appears back on our island, we stay until the dragon is slain. Then the village disappears again, and the dragon is once again alive."

"And whoever is in the village disappears with it?" Chance asked, his eyes darkening in disgust. "So, Myron is trying to trap us here?" They all felt a spark of anger at that thought.

"I don't know that for sure," Safron tried to placate them. "Eris may be fooling him into believing that it will free the village. When the curse first was cast, Myron lost the support of the village that he had always ruled with no opposition. All because he supported the stranger, regardless that the whole village had supported the stranger as well, the village blamed him." She gave a small smile. "At one time, Myron was a very good person and Archon but after the curse of Lapros, he changed."

"That still isn't a reason to try to trap us," Vanna protested, which surprised Telara. Vanna was usually the one trying to be the peacekeeper, sure everyone had a reason for how they acted.

"Who killed the dragon beforehand?" Pam asked Safron.

"Villagers and sometimes others that just happened to stumble onto our village from whatever time period they came from. One time, there was a large group with weapons that fired out balls of molten metal."

Tia shifted uncomfortably, and Telara could feel her discomfort. They were discussing the killing of Safron's husband as if discussing how to take apart a car or something. It sounded callous; yet, they needed the information if they were to leave this village before it disappeared.

Pam looked at Telara. "So, if Myron was told the Guardians killing the dragon would break the curse, he might believe it."

They all looked at each other suddenly uncomfortable. Could it be true? Aphrodite had made it sound as if that wasn't the case but then again, she was a Goddess and would say anything to suit her purpose. That is what all stories tell you. They looked at each other and then at Safron who wasn't looking at them but was staring off in the distance. Not that they could blame her; the Archon was trying to talk them into killing the dragon she loved as a man.

"Do you know how to break the curse?" Pam asked Safron gently.

Safron gave a sad smile. "I'm sorry, I wish I could help you, but I honestly don't know how to break the curse."

They stood up to head back to the Archon's when Vanna stopped and looked at Safron. "Not once tonight have you said the dragon's name, just called him the stranger. What is his name?"

The sigh that came from Safron was almost too soft to be heard. "Part of the curse, they said he no longer deserved to have a name." She looked up at them, and this time they could see the tears in her eyes. "Names have power you know, and they didn't want him to have any more power."

"So, no one can say his name?" Pam asked her eyes wide. Safron shook her head slowly before turning and heading back into her home with Spiro, who was waving to them making them promise to visit again soon.

14

___

"You have been speaking with Safron haven't you?"

They looked at each other not sure if they wanted to answer that question. Myron's voice held disdain in speaking Safron's name. They had just confronted him about the fact that every time someone has killed the dragon it had only caused the town to disappear with the dragon still alive. They had also pointed out the fact that if they killed the dragon, they would disappear with the town.

"She has nothing to do with this," Telara protested.

"Of course, she does!" His voice boomed off the stone walls in the sitting area. "She is in love with the dragon, believing one day he will once again become a human, and they can live happily ever after."

"Pretty much like you believe killing the dragon will stop the curse and you can win back the people and once again be adored," Pam stated staring at Myron with an extremely hard look.

"Can you blame me?" He angrily asked her, for once actually looking at Pam. "I want to free my people; she would keep us all stuck in this curse all for the hope of a hopeless dream."

"Yet, you have tried to kill the dragon many times and still the village is cursed with the dragon still alive," I.Q. spoke.

"But never has the dragon been killed by the Guardians." He grinned at them, a grin that reminded them of someone who was off his rocker. The Joker had nothing on that grin. "You will be the ones to free Lapros from this horrible curse. You will go down in history for this feat."

"All in your name right." Cole glared at Myron, all of them starting to feel dirty due to their association with the robust Archon standing before them with his ruddy red cheeks.

"And if it doesn't work? We will be stuck here in this town with no way out," Tia interjected.

"What does it matter? You will still be heroes." Myron looked at them; they could see the desperation in his eyes. "You won't be stuck here; I have been promised that if the Guardians slay the dragon the curse will be broken."

"I have a question." Pam stared at Myron who had gone back to refusing to look at her. "How did you know of the Guardians? No one in this village seemed surprised at their appearance and yet when this village was cursed there were no Guardians."

Telara stared at Pam then looked at Myron who suddenly had no interest at looking at any of them.

"It was Eris wasn't it?" Telara asked. She suddenly had a sinking feeling. She felt as if they were standing in the middle of a quicksand pit, that no matter where they stepped, they could be sucked down to a sandy death.

"The Goddess has decided to forgive us our betrayal. All we need to do is kill the source of that betrayal," he beseeched them to understand but all they knew was nothing felt right.

"You have to believe me; we need you to end this curse," he called after them when they started to walk away.

Telara stopped and turned to look at him. "Believe you? Why? You haven't been upfront with us about anything since coming here. Anything we have learned we have had to find out on our own through someone else."

His beady eyes narrowed on her. "So, you're just going to sentence us to live with this curse forever when you have the chance to end it?"

"No," Telara said, and Myron started to smile but stopped at her next words. "But neither will we run into this blind."

"If you don't kill the dragon, you have doomed Lapros," he hollered after them, but they just kept walking, no longer sure exactly what path to take but not wanting to be around Myron or even anyone from the village.

THEY FOUND A CLEARING JUST OUTSIDE THE TOWN BY A SMALL group of woods where there were several rocks they used as chairs. The sun had started to set, settling a purple hue across the land.

"I don't know about you guys, but I am more confused than when we first arrived," Chance said as he sprawled on the ground using a nice sized rock to lean his back on. They all nodded in agreement.

"Well, let's go over what we do know," Pam suggested.

"We know the town is cursed to be stuck in time." Vanna gave a sad smile.

"We know it was Eris and Ares who did it," Tia said looking up into the sky.

"All because of their own petty jealousies that someone

showed them how a god should truly be," Cole grumbled. His arms were crossed.

"This village was cursed by Eris and Ares because a stranger, whose name is no longer allowed to be spoken, came to the village and the villagers stopped their worship of Eris. The stranger was turned into a dragon that won't let anyone leave the town after they enter." Telara said, counting the items off on her fingers. She paused when something from their discussion with Safron registered, and she looked at them all. "We were always told when the darkness came to the land the Gods and Arions had banded together and fought them off."

The others nodded then Vanna looked at her with the same look of realization. "But according to Safron, these strangers were the ones who got rid of the darkness, not the Gods."

"Great!" Chance exploded. "More questions! Just what we need when we can't even figure out how to get out of this damn village!"

"Chance is right," Pam spoke up. They looked at her not sure what she meant. "We need to solve this mystery right here before worrying about others that we have no control over and won't if we can't get out of here."

"So, what is your suggestion?" Cole asked.

Pam shrugged and looked at Telara. "I think you are rubbing off on me." Telara stared at her confused as to what she was meaning. "I say we find this temple of Eris's and see if we can have a talk with the Goddess."

Cole and Chance jumped to their feet; their eyes lit up.

"Finally!" Chance exclaimed. The others laughed at them.

"What?" Cole protested. "Telara always gets to meet all the interesting people! It's about time we get to meet some."

Pam raised a brow at that then held up her hand before

Cole could say anything else. "I know what you mean but don't get your hopes up; she might not show."

"Only one way to find out," Telara said.

They started off towards the outskirts of town in the direction that Safron had looked when she spoke of the temple. Telara crossed her fingers that they would find it and hoped this wouldn't be a dead end. Otherwise, they might find themselves part of history, and not in a good way.

THEY FOUND THE TEMPLE AT THE END OF A PATH THROUGH THE woods. When they started up the steps Chad stumbled over a loose stone and ended up bumping into his brother which pushed him through the wooden door. He ended up landing on the stone floor on his backside. He glared at his apologetic brother while everyone helped him up. Looking around the temple, they saw cobwebs and dust covering almost all the tapestries and pedestals that were either bare or had some sort of statue or artifact on it.

"This place looks awful dingy for a temple." Cole sniffed then sneezed from all the dust.

"Didn't Safron say that Myron ordered daily offerings to her after they were cursed?" Vanna asked flinching at the sight of cobwebs in the doorway. Chance hurriedly swiped them out of the way before Telara could see them; while Vanna would flinch at the sight, they knew Telara would freak out.

"Definitely doesn't look like any of the temples we saw in the books back in class," Tia said looking around. "Where are the stone pillars holding up the ceiling with the towering statues?"

"Keep criticizing my temple, and I will turn you into a statue." The hard voice spoke from the darkness, startling them. As they watched, a raven-haired beauty with a very hard face stepped out from the shadows.

"Eris," Pam breathed and even Telara could hear the awe in her voice.

The woman smiled at her. "Very good, but who are you? There were only supposed to be seven Guardians."

Eris disappeared from where she was standing and appeared behind Pam looking her over before disappearing and appearing by Telara her brows furrowed as if they were a puzzle to her.

"And the Gods and Goddesses were supposed to be sleeping," Telara shot back.

She saw Pam roll her eyes signifying that once again she wasn't handling this very well. Considering this was only her third time addressing a Goddess, and the fact that she had never spoken to one before this adventure, she didn't think she was doing half bad.

Eris just shrugged a shoulder under the black cloth of her dress. The dress had a black leather belt, with something that resembled scales adoring the leather, which wrapped her waist. She gave a very unladylike snort.

"The Gods and Goddesses aren't sleeping." She laughed at the look of surprise on their faces. "Poor little mortals, being misled by your very own."

Her hands tightening into fists, Telara kept telling herself not to rise to the bait. And baiting them is precisely what Eris was doing.

"Think the Hercules show had her name right...Discord fits better than Eris."

Okay, Vanna's little quip had her smiling in agreement. Her

hands relaxed somewhat, something that wasn't missed by Eris whose face tightened in displeasure.

"Zeus has ordered everyone to stay in hiding."

They could tell she was not happy about it. Between her tone and posture, it was obvious she was highly ticked off about it.

"As if we have something to be ashamed of."

They watched her walk around the temple moving between the tattered tapestries that hung from the ceiling.

"We are Gods and Goddesses! We answer to no one!" She turned and looked at them. "We make the rules, and you mortals follow them; it is as simple as that." The last sentence was practically spat at them.

"And when someone doesn't follow them you curse them," Vanna told her angrily.

Telara almost laughed at the look of exasperation on Pam's face. Almost.

"Among other things," came Eris's haughty retort. Her eyes seemed to sparkle at the aggressive tone from Vanna.

"Be careful, Van. Remember, she likes to cause discord and anger. She might be looking at you like a smorgasbord."

They all nodded at Tia's comment and then looked abashed at Pam's raised eyebrow. They keep forgetting that she couldn't hear them, and they hated making her feel left out, so they did try to curb it. However, in tense situations like this, they couldn't help themselves.

"Mortals were created to worship us," Eris continued.

Her eyes never left Vanna causing I.Q. and Chad to stand closer to her, basically making sure they were between Eris and her. Rather than upset Eris, it seemed to make her smile even more.

"Over the years, they have forgotten this and so we either teach them a lesson or squash them like the bugs they are."

Telara saw Vanna tense. She was thankful the guys were right there to stop her from attacking Eris, just in case. Vanna might be the sweetest of them all, but her temper was the hottest. She frowned at Eris.

"So why not try to squash us? We aren't Gods," Telara said.

Eris tilted her head and looked at Telara. "No, you aren't," she acknowledged. "You are more of a means to an end." She gave them a smirk; her manner was really starting to grate on Telara's nerves.

"What do you mean?" Pam asked, and Eris turned her attention back to Pam.

"You don't have a connection to the others," Eris spoke staring at Pam, her expression one of either fascination or pure curiosity.

Pam shrugged. "I'm not a Guardian."

"Not a Guardian," Eris murmured. "So why are you here with them then?"

"She is a friend," Telara spoke up, stepping forward and garnering Eris's attention. This wasn't something she was trying for, but the way Eris spoke of Pam as if she didn't belong there was upsetting.

"A friend?"

"Yeah, Guardians are allowed friends you know." Chance crossed his arms staring at Eris. They thought they had gotten past the reputation from the previous Guardians and now this Goddess was making them feel as if they were right back there again.

Eris shrugged her shoulders, smirking at Chance, seeming to enjoy their frustrations. "Is that so? So, who else are your... Friends?" she inquired.

"What do you mean, who else are our friends?" Telara asked.

Telara looked around wondering exactly what was going on here. This situation was beginning to become very unreal. They were sitting there chatting with a Goddess, and the conversation was as enlightening as a burned-out bulb.

"I'm just curious about the Guardians is all."

Telara was really hating the snarky tone of her voice. It was as if Eris was mocking them, but why?

"She is just distracting us," Tia said, looking over at Telara. Pam groaned, and Eris laughed.

"Distracting you? Why on earth would a Goddess lower herself to distract a few kids?" They could hear the disdain in her voice but this time Telara was sure it was meant to rile them up. She was trying to distract them, but for what and why?

"You tell us," Telara said, but Eris just grinned. She had to control herself, so she didn't attempt to slap that grin off her face. She was pretty sure Guardian or not that would get her killed really quick.

"Well, I could be simply curious about the Guardians. After all, if you are unable to break the curse before the dragon dies you become a permanent resident of my little village."

Telara felt a very cold trickle run down her spine at Eris's words. The smirk she gave them didn't make her feel any better either.

"Or I could just be honestly curious as to why someone would go to such lengths to get you out of their way."

Was she trying to distract them or was there more to it? Telara wasn't sure, but it sure was beginning to make her extremely uncomfortable.

"Who wants us out of their way?" Telara asked.

"Is that truly the question you want answered?"

Telara had to take a deep breath before she screamed. Eris could make the Pope cuss on Sunday.

"This is a distraction, Telly," Pam spoke with conviction. "You can't trust anything she says."

"Can you trust anything anyone says?" Eris was having fun at their expense, and her eyes mirrored her glee.

"How do we break this curse?" Cole asked.

They could see from the look on Eris's face that she had no plans on telling them.

"It is as simple as saying a name."

Telara knew that singsong voice. Turning around, she saw she was right.

"Aphrodite," she breathed out. She could hear the gasps from the others as Aphrodite smiled and gave a small bow.

They all jumped as a glowing ball zoomed past them and hit the wall by Aphrodite who just laughed.

"Shut it, Barbie!" Eris snarled, her gloating smile of earlier now gone.

Aphrodite looked over at Pam with a look of interest. "You are pretty smart; the goth reject here is indeed trying to distract you."

"But why?" Pam asked.

Pam's face seemed to be devoid of color as she realized they were in a small building with two Goddesses who didn't seem to like each other. However, Pam wasn't letting that stop her from asking the questions that needed asking. Yeah, she could learn a lot from Pam Telara knew but then again Pam had many more years under her belt.

"If you had listened to her you would already know."

Telara groaned out loud. "Why can't you just answer a simple question without making more questions?"

Another light ball flew by them aimed for Aphrodite. This time, they could smell burnt hair. Aphrodite glared at Eris.

"You singed my hair you color deprived heathen."

She threw an energy ball. It exploded upon impact.

Eris dodged it and smirked at Aphrodite. "You throw like a girl."

"Move!" Pam shouted and ran to hide behind an upturned table with Tia closely following her. The others ran behind pedestals and overturned pieces of furniture that lay around the temple trying to avoid the volley of energy balls that were being thrown along with insults from the Goddesses.

They heard a groaning sound above them and looked up at the ceiling of the temple. They saw dust falling with each blast from the energy balls being tossed. Another groaning, and they saw some of the boards moving.

"Run!" Cole shouted.

They all headed towards the door, running out of the temple as the two Goddesses inside were still throwing energy balls and insults at each other.

They collapsed on the ground outside and watched as the temple shook and then fell in on itself.

"I don't suppose there is a chance that those two wouldn't have survived that?" Vanna asked. The others stared for just a minute before they laughed.

"Now that is just plain mean."

They turned and there stood Aphrodite standing there primping her hair that was suddenly looking perfect again. She looked down at them then turned around and looked at the woods behind her.

"And after I came here to warn you all about the threat to the dragon." She looked back at them. "Seems mortals aren't very appreciative."

With that, she disappeared.

"What threat to the dragon?" Tia asked her eyes wide. "If the dragon dies, we are stuck here."

"Are we sure about that?" I.Q. asked, ever the logical one.

"Even if we aren't, I don't know about you guys, but I'm not okay with a male who was cursed by the Gods dying if we can stop it." Telara stood up and looked around. "But how do we stop it? We don't even know where the dragon lives."

Pam was staring at the woods that Aphrodite had been looking at. Maybe she had been giving them a hint.

"Only one way to find out," Telara said and started walking. The others followed her, all wearing different expressions: unsure, scared, angry, and determined. Unsure exactly what was the truth and what wasn't, scared of failing everyone, angry about the Gods and how they liked to play with people's lives, and very determined to put an end to at least this one.

15
____

WHEN THEY GOT to the other side of the woods what they saw had them stopping in their tracks. There was a cave on the top of the hill. The mighty red dragon was roaring loudly as the village people swarmed the hill carrying scythes, pitch forks, and torches.

"My god! This looks like a scene out of the *Frankenstein* movie," Chance said, and the others nodded in agreement.

"No, leave him be!"

They looked and saw Safron standing there in front of the dragon trying to stop the village people from killing him.

"The dragon should be able to roast those people," Cole said but as they watched, the dragon only blew flames into the sky.

"He doesn't want to hurt the villagers," Vanna said.

They watched the scene unfold in front of them. It was like watching a car wreck: it was something so horrible, but they couldn't pull their eyes away.

"Yeah, well they don't seem to care about hurting him,"

Cole growled as a villager threw a pitchfork at the dragon. The dragon roared in pain as the pitchfork hit it in the head. "We can't just stand here; we have to do something."

They ran up the other side of the hill opposite of where the villagers were swarming to attack the dragon. They were running past the cave when they watched a villager shove Safron out of the way. They watched in horror as Safron fell to the side and over the edge of the hill to the jagged rocks below. The dragon roared in anger. They all cried out not believing what they were seeing. One or two of the villagers gasped out at this, but the others kept bearing down on the dragon with their weapons raised as if one of their own hadn't just fallen over the edge of the cliff.

Telara felt her eyes prick with tears and could feel the disbelief and sadness from the others. No way could she have survived a fall, not with the rocks at the bottom. Telara closed her eyes and swallowed hard.

"Look!"

Telara opened her eyes at Tia's gasp. There in front of them Safron was being raised back up to the hill by a tree. They all turned and looked at Vanna who was standing still staring in concentration. Vanna didn't move until Safron's feet touched the ground and she was steady. Then she looked at them and smiled.

"I didn't know if I could do it, but I had to try."

They all cheered and hugged her.

"Let's take care of the villagers now. Seems the odds just evened up," Chad laughed.

"Evened up? I think the odds just got stacked against the angry mob," said I.Q. Telara nodded in agreement with I.Q.

"I don't know why you guys didn't try this sooner," Pam

snorted then grinned as Vanna had a staff rise from the ground for her. Pam grabbed it and twirled it around with a very satisfied grin.

"Yeah, because we have always had our powers so being without them would be more alien than being with them," Telara snorted even though she was mentally asking herself the same question.

"Let's not hurt these people."

"Tell them that," Cole spoke back mentally as he ducked a shovel that was swung at him. He grabbed the handle and heated it up as the wood burned beneath his fingers. When the villager yanked back, the shovel fell to pieces. When the villager attempted to jump at Cole, he suddenly flew back falling to the ground several feet away from a giant gust of wind.

"You're welcome." Tia grinned and then turned to send a few more villagers soaring through the air.

Chance had just drenched several villagers, who spent more time slipping in the mud as they kept trying to get past Chance and to the dragon. He was so busy laughing at them calling them the three stooges that he didn't see the villager who was sneaking up on him.

"Chance!" Telara hollered, but the villager managed to swing his shovel and connect with the side of Chance's head. Telara jumped away from the fray she was in. With barely a thought, she sent the villager over ten feet away where he landed in an unconscious heap. The three stooges who were no longer being pushed down by Chance's water stood up and looked like they were going to advance on him, but they all ended up being thrown together and hitting their heads together before sliding down unconscious in the mud.

Between Tia's wind and Telara's telekinesis, they weren't getting up anytime soon.

Telara knelt by Chance, whose eyes were rolling, but he was conscious. The shovel had bruised him, and there was a small cut, but the damage wasn't lethal.

"Stay down," Telara told Chance. He nodded as she stood up and looked back at the battlefield. The villagers were still coming at the dragon while Pam, Safron, and the Guardians fought them off.

The dragon roared out in pain, flames lighting the night sky, as a villager managed to connect with his hind leg with his scythe. Telara managed to knock him away before he could get another swipe in. The trees and bushes around them joined in the fray, roots coming out of the ground tripping villagers and knocking them back. The villagers farm-like weapons were freezing in their hands or they would be dropping them from jolts of electricity that would travel along the metal shocking them.

No matter how hard they fought, the villagers kept coming. Trying to not do any lethal damage to them was making this fight even harder. Pam managed to sweep several villagers off their feet but, if not for Tia and her winds, she would have joined Chance on the sidelines.

"There has got to be a way to end this." Tia could feel the agreement from the others, but she seriously wasn't sure how to do that without doing some major damage to these idiots. They were following the orders of their Archon who was standing off to the back shouting at them to keep fighting. *"He would make one hell of a politician, standing in the back away from danger while sending everyone else into the battle."*

"His name!"

Telara looked back at Cole. He had had just grabbed the torch of a villager who was attempting to hit him with it. This caused the flame to shoot out startling the villager into letting go and running.

"What?"

"The dragon's name. Safron said names have power, and Aphrodite said breaking the curse is as easy as saying a name."

Could it be that simple? Telara turned back to toss a few more villagers when Cole spoke again.

"Telara, I am sure of it. The song that had me in a trance, what Safron and Aphrodite said. I need his name; only I can free him."

"You?"

"Just trust me, please."

She could hear the conviction behind his words. While she was still very skeptical, she knew he believed what he said, and she believed in her friends. The others hadn't said a thing, but she could feel them paying close attention to their conversation as they fought off the villagers.

"Okay, but how do we get his name?"

"Safron."

"She can't speak his name," Telara protested as she tried erecting a force field around the dragon and her friends. Unfortunately, she was finding it more draining than she thought, so she had to settle with just pushing the villagers away from the dragon and her friends.

"But she knows what it is."

"How will that help us if she can't speak it out loud?"

"Telly, we talk all the time without speaking out loud; it is there in her mind. We just have to get it."

"Just have to get it?" Telara stopped and stared at him not believing he had just made it sound so simple.

"It can be, Telly. I have faith in you. You can do it."
"We all do."

Telara couldn't believe it; they all spoke at once, and she felt the confidence they had in her when she had none. She had never attempted to get into someone else's head before. Her palms were sweaty at the thought. She shook her head when Pam looked at her; she knew Pam knew they were mind-speaking again, but she couldn't fill in their friend right now; she was too nervous thinking about what she was about to attempt to do.

"Fine, but you guys will have to keep these guys off of me."

They told her not to worry. Of course, she was worried but not about that. She took in a deep breath and concentrated on Safron, on projecting her thoughts into her mind.

"Safron!"

Safron slammed her hands over her ears, and Telara grimaced as she realized that she had just yelled right into Safron's mind.

"Sorry."

Safron looked at her with eyes wide and her face one of amazement.

"Yes, I just spoke to you mentally," Telara told her trying to keep her projected voice low. She could feel her friends there with her, listening in as they fought to keep the villagers from hurting the dragon while at the same time not hurting the villagers who were being egged on by Myron the Loudmouth.

"Kill the beast! Break this curse!"

She really wanted to gag that man but instead she concentrated on talking with Safron.

"We need the name of the dragon when he was a man."
"God."

She glared at Cole who instantly looked contrite. She turned back to Safron who shook her head and mouthed she couldn't say his name.

"I know, Safron. I don't want you to say it. I want you to think it. Just remember it in your mind and think the name."

She saw Safron nod at her, close her eyes, and Telara heard the name loud and clear. She looked at Cole who nodded and ran towards the cave. He slammed his hand on the fire symbol and shouted out the name loud and clear. Telara was blinded by a bright light and then…nothing.

Telara opened her eyes, using her hand to shield them from the blaring sun. Sun? She looked around and saw her friends all shaking their heads and looking around. The villagers were gone, and it was daytime. How long had they been out?

Cole helped Chance to stand. Chance leaned heavily on Cole letting them know it hadn't been a dream. Vanna screamed, and they all came running to where she was standing staring down at the ground, pointing at something. They all jumped when they saw a skull laying there.

"What the…?"

Cole was cut off when Tia nudged him and pointed over to the edge of the hill. A man knelt there on the ground by some bones with multi-colored scarves adorning them.

"Safron?" Telara felt her stomach tighten as she felt the sadness from all around them, even from Pam. They had only known her a short time, a very short time, but still they felt sad seeing those scarves and colorful bracelets.

The male moved from his position and stood up, turning to look at them. He had red flaming hair weaved within the sandy brown hair that curled around his neck to his shoulders. He had to be at least 6 feet tall, if not more. He towered over them as he walked towards them. His blue eyes reminded her of Lucius's icy blue ones. They were a huge contrast from the fiery tints in his hair. It was hard to believe that not that long ago he had been a fire breathing dragon.

"Thank you for breaking the curse." His voice could only be described as husky and gruff sounding. This may have been due to his being a flame throwing dragon for how many millenniums they didn't know.

They looked around them at the bones as they started to realize what had happened. They broke the curse, and the villagers were dead.

"So, we broke the curse and killed everyone," Vanna said feeling very morose.

"You didn't kill anyone," the male told her. "You freed them; they died long ago, but that curse kept their souls from leaving."

They looked at each other. His words still didn't make them feel any better as they thought of little Spiro. He was so young.

"How long has it been?" he asked.

Their brows furrowed at his question before Pam answered him.

"It is the 21st century," she told him gently. Now he was the one who looked confused. "Trust me," she continued. "It has been a very long time."

He gave a slow nod and looked around them at the bones that littered the hillside outside his cave.

"Well, the dragon's cave which was his cave but now..." Telara

shook her head and heard the snickers of the others in her head. Too confusing.

"Maybe you should tell me what has happened during my absence while I get my bearings."

They nodded, moving quickly away from the bones that littered the hillside and moving over towards the cave.

16

"May I see one of these crystals?"

They had been sitting around the outside of the cave telling him what they knew about what had happened since he had been cursed. Well, they told him the only version they knew. After what Safron had told them, they weren't sure if that was exactly what had happened.

Since he already knew about the darkness coming to the land, they told him how the Gods had created Sanctuary for the magical creatures of Greece to protect them from the darkness and of the big battle where the Gods and Goddesses had fought alongside the Arions to beat the darkness. He snorted at hearing that, but they continued saying how the Gods and Goddesses had seemed to disappear after the battle. He grinned at hearing that, and Telara felt shivers crawl up her spine. The others looked uncomfortable except for Cole who was staring at the man in wonder.

Then they told him about the crystals and how only descendants from the Gods could work the crystals. He frowned at that. They told him the story of the Guardians, and they watched as his face hardened and his lips thinned into a tight line.

I.Q. stood up. "But they have not worked since we got here." He went to unstrap his Crim from his wrist and to everyone's surprise the watch became I.Q.'s bow in his hand. "Er...Well, they didn't at first."

He handed the Crim to the man. As soon as he touched the metal part of the bow, it turned back into its original form, which was not the wristwatch that normally adorned I.Q.'s wrist.

"Where did these come from?" The man looked at the crystal, turning it around in his hand and examining it with great interest.

"No one knows exactly." Vanna watched him. "All we do know Mr...?" Vanna paused as she attempted to call him by name. They had heard his name from Safron through their mental link with her, and Cole had even shouted it out loud, but something was stopping her from saying it. She looked up at the man, her face full of confusion.

The others attempted as well before looking over at Cole, who opened his mouth only to discover that the name he had hollered out earlier now stuck in his throat.

The man gave a dry humorless laugh. "Seems the Gods have a sick sense of humor. I still don't know how the boy managed to say my name out loud; could be their idea of a joke." The man shrugged then continued, "You may call me Kull; that is what little Spiro used to call me."

They each gave a sad smile at hearing Spiro's name.

"All we know is that only one with the blood of a God or Goddess can operate them," Vanna answered his earlier question.

They all gasped as I.Q.'s Crim glowed in his hand then changed into a spear red as fire.

He gave them a grim smile before handing the glowing spear to I.Q. The Crim changed back into its watch form.

"Hmmm," he murmured before looking at them once again. "You are all children of the Greek Gods?" he asked with a thoughtful look.

"Well, descendants of the Greek Gods," Pam told him. "There are actually no more direct children of the Gods or Goddesses as they have not been seen for so long."

"And they sent you to break this curse of theirs?" His tone was skeptical as was the look he gave them, causing them to squirm.

"Actually, no," Telara admitted. "We have never spoken to any Gods or Goddess before coming to this town. Uh...Long story," she said when his brow raised, but he held up his hand.

"No need. So, how did you discover this town?"

Telara pointed to the symbol still on the entrance to the cave. "Your symbol."

He looked at the symbol then back at her, and they could see the question in his eyes. She explained about the symbols that appeared on her bedroom ceiling back in Sanctuary. He looked real interested in that but didn't say anything until she told him about also seeing the symbols on buildings in the town.

"How did you know about the symbols on the buildings in a town you have never seen?" he questioned her, so they went on to explain the concert. They discovered it was very hard to explain a concert to a man who has been stuck back in the dark ages for so long.

"It was basically a vision given to us by what you would

call an oracle sung by a bard," Pam tried to explain, and this explanation he seemed to understand.

"And the names of the oracle and bard?" he asked.

"Actually, it is the same person," Vanna said softly.

"Really?" He seemed to ponder this and then asked, "Well, does this person have a name?"

When they told him the name, he brought his hand to his chin rubbing it absently in thought. "I wonder…" he said softly to himself and then looked at each of them with that searching gaze that made them all feel a bit uncomfortable. Even Cole felt a bit uneasy, the wonder seemed to have waned and now he was as unsure as the others. "And who are your godly parents?"

"We don't really know." Chad scuffed his feet in the dirt.

"How can you not know your parents from whom you received your powers?"

"As we have told you, the Gods do not show themselves anymore. Well, unless you count our experience last night and even then, it wasn't like they were very helpful," Tia said in a defensive tone, her arms crossed as she looked at him.

"You are telling me that the Greek Gods have disappeared completely and no longer meddle in the affairs of mortals whom they consider their playthings?" The sardonic tone in his voice showed his disbelief in that information. "Now, that I find hard to believe."

"Well, you can believe it," Telara told him hotly. "All they have left us is more questions and not enough answers. All we know is that we were given these powers to defeat the Magine that is due to waken anytime."

"Magine? Who is this Magine?"

"It is not a who but a what," Pam told him. "It is another Shadow Creature that the Shadow Master created. It is so powerful that only the powers of the Guardians can defeat it. With no Guardians to defeat the Magine, it will destroy all in its path and encompass the word in a darkness that will never end."

"Guardians?"

"That would be...Us," Vanna finished holding out her hands. At his look of disbelief, they all felt suddenly inadequate.

"Guardians hmmmm?" He looked each of them over and gave a slow shake of his head. "And you children are the Guardians that will defeat this Magine?" His tone sounded disbelieving, and Telara felt herself bristle at it.

"These *children* just released you from the curse you have been under for how many centuries?" Telara practically growled at him, her patience gone. He just looked at her with a mocking smile on his face that made her itch to smack it off.

"*Telara!*" Tia cautioned her, and Kull's smiled widened as if he had heard her warning.

Telara looked around and realized that in her anger her power was starting to grow. There were small rocks and twigs swirling around her. The others were staring at the swirling stones and twigs. She took a deep breath to calm herself down, and everything dropped to the ground with soft thuds.

"Very nice." Kull smiled at her. "I wonder..."

"What?" Telara asked him.

He didn't answer her but looked over at the bones with the colored scarves and bracelets. "You spoke of Sanctuary where others such as yourself lived."

"Yeah."

They looked at each other not sure what he was getting at.

"Ran by a charismatic male named Lucius."

"Again, yeah. Why?" Kull was getting on Telara's nerves.

"The name sounds familiar." He smiled at her and rose from his position on a boulder.

"I don't think he is that old." Chance shrugged.

Kull nodded. "You are probably right." He stood up and walked over to the bones. "I need to give them a proper burial." He looked back at them. "You are more than welcome to help but if you choose not to, I will understand."

"We will help," Telara said feeling her eyes prick with tears. "They deserve it, and we would like to give Safron and Spiro a final goodbye."

Kull nodded at her, and they all set about giving the entire town a proper burial.

THEY STOOD TOGETHER STARING AT THE GRAVES THEY HAD SPENT the rest of the day digging. They were now all filled in with makeshift tombstones thanks to Vanna who was able to somehow carve into the stones the names of each person. They had all said their goodbyes and now watched as Kull knelt by Safron's grave with his head bowed. They all turned away to give him some sense of privacy with his beloved.

"Alpha Leader come in."

They all started as they heard Claw's voice. They glanced at Pam as they suddenly realized that Sanctuary must be going nuts having no contact with them for the past several days. They all groaned thinking about Ira and Lucius' anger over their illegal mission.

"Looks like it is time to face the music," Chance grumbled.

"Alpha Leader here, Claw. Sorry about the delay. How bad is the situation?" Pam stood ramrod as she waited for the tongue lashing that Claw was sure to relish in giving her.

"Delay? Gee missing me already Alpha Leader?" Claw's mocking voice came back to them. "And the situation be the same as it was thirty minutes ago when we last spoke. Ira has informed Zeke that as soon as your patrol is done, he will be wanting to see you in his office."

They all looked at each other. "What do you mean thirty minutes, Claw?" Telara asked, her brow furrowed.

"Wow…Guardian Leader doesn't even know how to tell time. Ye know when the big and little hand be on the twelve, it be twelve o'clock. When the big hand moves down to point at the six at the bottom that means it be twelve thirty. That would be meaning thirty minutes have passed."

Telara gritted her teeth but before she could give him a retort to blow back his hair, Pam held up her hands.

"All right, Claw. Sorry we have been a bit distracted. We will discuss everything when we get back to Sanctuary." They all heard Claw's very amused chuckle. "Just get ready to transport us plus one back to base, Claw."

"Plus one? What is going on?"

Pam grinned, looking back to where they had left Kull kneeling by Safron's grave, but he was no longer there. They looked around but he was nowhere to be seen, just all the graves they had dug with their headstones. They looked at each other not sure what to do. Kull had left them with many unanswered questions even though they had answered his.

"Never mind, Claw. It will just be us. Ready for transport."

Pam shook her head, and they didn't need to be able to read her mind to know that she was just as confused as they were.

"Git yer shades ready, ladies and gents."

They all groaned realizing they had left them back at the Archon's home. They were not sure whether to be surprised when their shades suddenly appeared in their hands. They stared at each other for a few seconds before quickly putting them on just as the light surrounded them and transported them back to Sanctuary.

Everyone was sitting in the Gamma Squad's sitting area in their quarters. All the factions were there from the Alphas to the Omegas, even Carmen was there. They were all listening as Pam and the Guardians told them what had happened. Pam and the Guardians did keep some things to themselves; the fact that Safron's story and the story everyone had been told didn't coincide was something they didn't want to speak about. Not before they were able to find out all the answers. They didn't want to create anymore chaos than there already was.

"Yeah, let's leave that up to Discord," Cole's sarcastic reply spoke in their minds.

"Eris," I.Q. corrected him.

"I think Discord fits her better," Chance agreed.

They all kind of shrugged in agreement. The sound of someone clearing their throat reminded them that not everyone here had the ability to mind speak.

"Sorry."

The other factions laughed, except for Carmen and the Betas. Although Telara was sure she saw one or two of them crack a small smile. This being the first time Telara had seen any of them, they understood what Pam was talking about. Carmen had an air about her that made it seem as if she thought she was better than you. Her reddish auburn hair was perfect as was her makeup, and Telara was sure her clothes didn't have one wrinkle.

"So ye be saying that not only did the Gods curse this town but they also spoke at ye?"

Telara nodded at Claw, who seemed to be processing this information, as were the others. Out of everything that they had told them, this seemed to hit everyone the hardest. Telara was starting to feel uncomfortable, as if that fact was going to be another reason for everyone to dislike the Guardians.

"So, after all these years of us risking our lives in service of the Gods and Goddesses, they finally show themselves to the heroic Guardians," Carmen stated, and her voice showed her displeasure. Enough that Telara turned on her before Pam could step in.

"You want to talk to them then go for it! It isn't a walk in the park, and I honestly couldn't care less if I speak to another God or Goddess for as long as I live." Telara's voice was tight, and the air around her sparked.

Carmen looked her over; her look was one of disdain. "And yet they chose you to speak to."

"That is enough, Carmen!" Pam's voice cut across the room as she stared at Carmen who glared right back at her.

"Oh, that is right! You are one of the Guardian's pets now."

They all looked at each other at the venom in Carmen's voice. They remembered Pam telling them that Carmen was worse than she was but, never having met her officially, they were unprepared for the bitterness that spewed from Carmen.

From the look on Pam's face, Telara wondered if she wouldn't be the one having to stop a fight from breaking out. Of course, she would love to see Carmen's perfect face rearranged. Vanna nudged her with a frown; their peacekeeper was very disapproving of Telara's thoughts. Telara shrugged and turned back to watch the showdown.

"Either have something productive to put forward on this conversation, sit down with your mouth shut, or you know where the door is." Pam's gaze was hard, and there was no doubt in anyone's mind why she led the Alpha faction. She held herself tall and not once did she wilt under the disdainful look of the Beta Leader.

Carmen glared at Pam then looked around. For a minute, Telara was sure she was going to storm out of the room but, with pressed lips, she sat back down.

"So, anyone know who this Kull is...or was?" Gabe spoke up and winked at Vanna whose cheeks went a shade of pink.

"Is," Cole spoke with conviction, and the others looked at him. "He is alive."

"Okay, so who is he?" Brie looked at him.

Cole shrugged and looked at Telara who also shrugged but answered. "That is the puzzle that we mean to unravel."

Claw opened his mouth to say something but whatever it was they would have to wait to find out. The sounds of the Shadow alarms whistled and screamed all around them along with the lights that flashed.

"Back to business, gents." Claw grinned as everyone scattered to their posts.

"Welcome home," Chad muttered as they followed Pam and the other Alphas to the Control Room to suit up and do what Guardians do.

17

———

"SET 'EM UP, JOE!"

Tia and Telara rolled their eyes at Cole's and Chad's robust exclamation as they entered Czaar's Cantina. They had had a successful battle with the Shadows. They had even managed to capture a few that were now in holding cells and getting ready to be de-shadowed. Vanna and Tia didn't want to take off their new uniforms they had been given: shiny purple stretch suits that resembled the out-in-space look that graced I.Q.'s Stargazer. Now, it was time for some relaxing at Czaar's Cantina before going to the bungalow for the night.

"Set what up?"

They looked at each and laughed at Joe, who was one of the Beta faction members. He had a very likable personality; in their book, he was all right. Which was odd considering whose faction he was in.

"It is a saying from a very old country song," Tia explained laughing as his dark eyes turned towards her still confused. "It basically means he is asking for a round of drinks."

Rather than appeasing Joe, his eyes got wide, and he

looked at the guys with a dark look; considering Joe's dark features and deep voice, he looked pretty menacing. "I am not paying for a round of drinks, boys."

They held up their hands in surrender.

"Not saying you're paying for the drinks; we are calling the bartender Joe."

Daphne, who had slithered out from behind the bar with a tray of drinks for them, all non-alcoholic of course, cleared her throat while glaring at Cole and Chad. Before they could explain they weren't literally calling her a guy's name, she slammed the drinks down on the table and slithered away.

"Way to go boys," Telara said picking up her mug and watching Silest's signature punch trickle down the sides of his glass. It was spilling over after having been so rudely slammed onto the table. They all chuckled at the look of chagrin on their faces. It was an honest mistake when you grew up outside of Sanctuary. Daphne, the bartender and resident Dracaena, could be heard noisily slamming cups behind the bar.

Joe just shook his head, and they all sat down to enjoy some punch before they retired for the night. It was nice chatting about their battle and how no one had been injured. It was good to basically just goof around for a few hours.

Telara sat there silently drinking her punch, looking around the tavern, and just watching. People watching is what they called it. She was watching her friends, deep in thought. Cole, Claw, and Gabe were standing around the game table watching a few satyrs playing as the lights were lighting up with cheers and jeers from the crowd. Rainbow ball, the game of chance where you attempt to connect your ball with a bumper of the same color. Also the game where Vanna beat Claw months ago. Serdita was in the corner with her Chenras creating a very melodic melody. Pam and Gage were at the bar chatting with Daphne who was still sending dirty looks at Chad and Cole.

Telara felt more at home here than she did back in Dragoon. They had only been here a short time but already it was their home and family.

Some shouting had everyone turning and there, zooming along the floor in his little car, was Fritz. He ran the car up a little ramp that was next to the bar that Telara hadn't noticed before. She watched as he zoomed up the ramp and landed on the bar top with a squeal of his tires, stopping right in front of Daphne. He held out a tiny cup that she filled with a roll of her eyes.

It was several hours later before they ambled back to their bungalow, none of them ready to call it a night. Vanna wanted to stop in the Static Room and see Streak, the silver squirrel she had adopted last time they were here, who rode on her shoulder to her room. It seemed he had missed her as well. In her room, Telara grinned as she saw her little squiggly friends playing on the ceiling. Home was her last thought before she drifted off to sleep.

SHE OPENED HER EYES AND TURNED OVER IN THE BED. LEANING against the wall of her bedroom was Zach. She sat up and gave him an accusing look.

"Where have you been? We could have used you back in Lapros."

"I couldn't."

"Why?" Out of all answers she expected, that wasn't one of them.

Zach walked over to the window that looked out over the

lake where the water lay still as if sleeping. "Lapros existed in a time where I didn't."

"What do you mean you didn't exist?"

He looked over at her and grinned. "You think I'm that old?"

She opened her mouth then suddenly she understood a lot of things that had them confused. "That was why our Crims didn't work." I.Q. and Pam had been right.

He nodded at her.

"But our powers did! How could they work when our Crims didn't?"

He opened his mouth but then shut it. She wasn't having any of that though. "Oh no you don't. You aren't going to tell me half a story and then leave me hanging. We get enough of that as it is."

He sighed. "I can only tell you what I think."

She snorted. "That is better than silence."

He gave a wry grin. "The Crims wouldn't work if they didn't exist at that time but if your godly parents lived at that time then your powers that you got from them would."

She listened, and she had to admit it did make sense. "Okay, that makes sense."

He smiled at her. Suddenly, they were no longer in her room but on the grassy shore of Mermaid Lake. She smiled; this was the spot where she and the others liked to sit. Seemed they weren't the only ones who liked it.

"I only brought you here because it seems to calm you."

She looked at him. "You can read minds?" He gave a shrug then something else occurred to her. "Is there a reason the lake will have to calm me?"

He shrugged again and sat down by the tree, patting a

patch of grass for her to sit. After a few seconds, she grudgingly sat down and stared at the water.

"You have some questions for me, right?" He grinned. "Or am I mistaken?"

"You are not mistaken."

He shrugged. "So, ask."

"Last week..." She paused as she realized that time hadn't passed while they had been in Lapros, so she amended what she was going to say. "A few days ago, you told me if we went on that journey, we would lose something very important to us, but we didn't lose anything."

He chuckled. "That is a statement, not a question."

She glowered at him which just made him chuckle more. "You know what I meant and don't even attempt to try a language barrier. I think you speak better English than Cole or Chad now." And considering that when they had first met, he couldn't speak a word of English that was saying something.

He gave a nod of his head as if saying thank you then laughed when her brow furrowed even more before sobering up.

"You did lose something, just something you never knew you had."

She groaned. "Gods, you must be related to Lucius somehow."

He looked at her with a confused look. "Related?"

"You both like to talk in riddles," she groused at him, but he just shrugged and winked at her.

"Sorry, I don't mean to. Maybe he and I had the same teacher." He shrugged. "I will try to be better."

She gave a disbelieving snort, and he chuckled.

"So, what did we lose then?"

"You lost your protection," he told her, and the tone of his voice sounded so ominous that it sent chills down her spine.

"Protection? What do we need protection from?"

"The Gods."

"Wait! We are their descendants, their Guardians. We were chosen by them for this…whatever you want to call it. We didn't ask for it," Telara protested feeling even more confused than ever. "Why do we need protection from the Gods?"

"The story of the Gods, the unknowns, the Shadows, and Sanctuary that you were told at first is not completely accurate."

She gave a snort. "Starting to figure that out for myself." She was beginning to wonder if anything Lucius told her was true.

"Are you saying you don't want me to tell you what I know?"

His calm words had her thinking of Lucius again, but she bit back that retort and apologized instead.

"It isn't Lucius's fault and confronting him would do no good."

"But we need answers," she protested.

"So, find them."

He grinned sideways at her, and she could have sworn she saw a twinkle in his eyes. Ever since their first meeting, his eyes always looked dull as if there was no life there.

"How when Lucius won't tell us anything?" She groaned then looked at him.

"Lucius is bound by a promise, one that he made to protect your lives."

Great, she grumbled to herself. In other words, she couldn't badger Lucius for information now. If she caused him guilt over not being able to tell her anything because he was protecting them, she would feel awful. Then she got an idea.

"How about you?" When he gave her a questioning look, she nodded. "Why can't you tell us what is going on? Why we would need protection from Gods and Goddesses who are our ancestors? Or are you bound by a promise as well?"

He gave a half smile and shook his head. "I am bound by no promise; neither the Gods nor the Goddesses of this world have any hold over me."

She perked up at hearing that. "So, you can tell me then?"

He gave a slow shake of his head. "I wish I could, but I can't tell you that which I don't know. What happened was before my time; I am just along for the ride." He gave a grin.

"If it happened before your time then how do you know the story isn't accurate?" Was constant confusion part of being a Guardian?

"I hear things but not enough to know the full story, just enough to know what is being said is what the Gods want their descendants to believe." He looked into her eyes. "I believe you seven will be the ones to discover all the secrets that the Gods are hiding. I warn you to be cautious with your findings. If the wrong people find out what you are doing, then your lives will be in danger."

She almost snorted at that. After all, the Guardians were born to fight and die basically. "Are you telling me we shouldn't keep looking for answers?"

He grinned even bigger. "Oh no, not at all. I am looking forward to you shattering the bubble the Gods and Goddesses have surrounded themselves in for so long. But you need to be cautious with who you share your information with. There is a reason the past Guardians were considered anti-social; their powers weren't the only reasons."

She stood up. "I am not about to let our powers isolate us from our friends."

He shook his head. "You misunderstand me. I am not saying that is the way it should be, just explaining why the other Guardians weren't so sociable."

"You speak as if you knew them." Telara looked down at him, but he was still watching the water's surface.

"To discover the truth of what truly happened, you must discover the truth of the unknown Gods and Goddesses. Discover their story, and you might be able to change yours."

Before she could answer, he disappeared right before her. Before she could blink, she was back in her room.

Would her life ever get back to normal? Did she even know what normal was anymore?

"CARETAKER."

Lucius was standing in his office looking out the window that overlooked the Static Room. His Guardians had come to call it the Power Room. The name had grown on him as did the children he had watched grow into young adults.

His visitor with the gravelly voice, from living as a dragon for centuries after centuries, was expected. As was the conversation they were about to have. Next to him on the table sat a decanter filled with amber liquid to sooth both their palates.

"Are you going to just stand there or are you going to acknowledge my presence?" The irritation was evident in the bite of his tone.

"I see your patience hasn't improved during your years of confinement." Lucius couldn't help the smile; it was good to hear his old friend's voice.

"Confinement? You call being cursed as a dragon confinement?" Kull growled even sharper.

Lucius turned to look at Kull. "Would you rather me call it something else? Vacation? Or maybe a time out?"

Kull's eyes changed from blue to fiery red. His body practically glowed red, causing the temperature in the room to rise quickly. Lucius knew he was baiting him, but it had been so long he truly couldn't help himself. Through the years, living at the Sanctuary in which ever land it decided to take them, chasing after the Guardians, he had always felt so alone. Missing the ones that were the closest to him.

"Control that temper, Kull, before I do it for you." He sat down in one of the leather chairs and gestured for Kull to join him. There were two glasses on the table, and he picked up one of them. "Why don't we just sit down like old friends and discuss this calmly?"

"Friends? Is that what we are?" Kull's voice still held animosity, but his eyes were once again blue, and the temperature had cooled considerably. He even moved to the chair and grabbed the glass full of the amber liquid and took a drink. "What is this?"

"Just something to cool that temper of yours." Lucius watched Kull take a seat. "Why wouldn't we be friends?" Lucius answered his first question.

"I have been stuck as a damn dragon with no help from anyone while you have been living free," Krull growled and gestured around the office with the desk, chairs, and pictures on the wall.

Lucius stared at the very irate male whose burly frame dwarfed the chair he sat in, his blue eyes turning icy cold. "Free? While you have been imprisoned as a dragon for being such a hothead, I had to watch while the others were cursed one by one. If not for my diplomatic skills that you like to demean, I would have been imprisoned as well."

"And yet, here you sit." Kull's tone was as combative as his demeanor. "I have to ask myself why."

"Simple, we needed someone who could keep their calm to remain uncursed."

"And who decided that you would be the one?"

"Marsella."

Kull stilled at her name. "Is she…" He couldn't bring himself to say the words, but Lucius just nodded.

Lucius looked out the window down to the Static Room. "She wanted someone to protect your children from the pettiness of the Gods and Goddesses." Kull's head jerked around, and Lucius nodded at the shock in his eyes. "Yes, your children. The same ones who freed you from your imprisonment."

Kull sat there silently staring into his drink, more subdued than Lucius had ever seen him. Not that he could blame him; that was a lot to process. "The others?"

Lucius gave a sad shake of his head; he couldn't bring himself to speak of their fates. Especially Marsella.

Kull's head fell heavily into his hands as he shook it back and forth in disbelief. "What do we do?"

"Have faith."

"Faith? In what?"

"The Guardians."

"Those children?" Kull raised his head staring at Lucius as if he had lost his mind.

"Those children are your descendants," Lucius reminded him.

"They are kids who know nothing of their true heritage."

"That is not of their own doing," Lucius defended his Guardians, and Kull's eyes narrowed on him.

"You seem awful protective of these children."

Lucius nodded. "I am. They have come a long way in a very short time."

"They have no idea what they are facing," Kull protested.

"Give them a chance; they might surprise you." Lucius smiled. "Actually, I am positive they will surprise you."

Kull snorted at that.

"They saved your sorry ass, didn't they?"

Kull stared at Lucius before finishing his drink in one swallow. "I should have killed you like I planned on when I came here."

Lucius just smiled. "You probably should have."

ABOUT THE AUTHOR

T.L. Shively is an award-winning author who plays mom and wife with a daytime job but after hours you will find her knee-deep in gnomes, fairies, and all things fantasy. She loves when her imagination takes her places she hasn't been, then she writes them down on paper so she can share them.

OTHER BOOKS BY TL SHIVELY

The Sanctuary Guardian Series

The Secret Sanctuary

(Book One)

The Independence Mine Disaster

(A short story prequel)